THE WONDERS OF LIFE AND ALL THAT IT HOLDS

JACQUELYN HIGHTOWER

ARCHWAY PUBLISHING

Archway Publishing books may be ordered through booksellers or by contacting:

Archway Publishing
1663 Liberty Drive
Bloomington, IN 47403
www.archwaypublishing.com
844-669-3957

ISBN: 978-1-6657-4761-5 (sc)
ISBN: 978-1-6657-4762-2 (e)

Library of Congress Control Number: 2023914273

Print information available on the last page.

Archway Publishing rev. date: 09/19/2023

Thanks to Archway Publishing for opening doors and allowing the third book to be published from thoughts and memories, along with creativity waiting to be shared with readers.

Thanks to Cedar Hill Library, Midlothian Town Crossing, Grimes Park, and Hill Side Village Shopping Center. Much meditational time was spent in all locations getting the book together.

Last but not least, Excel Publishing I made it through.

ELAINE AND HER FAMILY GO ON VACATION TO NEW YORK

HI, MY NAME IS ELAINE. I live in Dallas, Texas (South Oak Cliff). I have attended several elementary schools, and neither was my favorite to talk about. I attended school like a typical 10-year-old. I stayed to myself. I did not know many friends. When I come home from school, I do my homework and find things to do around the house.

My Mom and Dad promised me if I continued to make good grades for the second semester, they would surprise me with a vacation trip.

Saturday, Dad took Mom and me to the ice cream store. We shared a giant banana split. Dad mentioned we would be taking a vacation trip in a few weeks to New York. We will be there for a week.

"Yeah, thanks, Dad," Elaine said.

"I always wanted to take a trip to New York. Now we have an opportunity to go sightseeing," Elaine said.

"I am so excited to see something other than Texas," Elaine said.

My family has already made arrangements for the trip. We will be staying at the Hampton Inn, close to where there are a lot of tourist attractions.

Elaine attended school for two weeks with the excitement of taking a trip to New York. She was glowing with joy.

It was time to leave for the airport. Mom checked my luggage and ensured I had packed enough for a few days.

Dad had already dropped Sam, our dog, off at the kennel.

We left DFW and arrived at La Guardia Airport. We picked up our luggage with no problem. We exited the airport to see if a courtesy car awaited our arrival. We looked and waited 10 minutes. We did not see the limousine. Dad went back to the airport to find the hotel's courtesy phone. The courtesy phones are on the wall in the back corner. Dad found the phone for the Hampton Inn. Dad called the hotel. A person answered and asked how they could help him. Dad requested a courtesy car for the Hines family to pick up at the La Guardia Airport. No one is here. The person on the line said let me transfer you to the driver. The driver answered, and Dad asked if the Hines family were on the list for pick up from the La Guardia airport. The driver said he was leaving and would arrive in about 10 minutes. Dad finished the call and went back outside with the family.

A driver approached us while we all were standing near the curve. He had a sign that said Hampton Inn the Hines family. The driver got out of the car and introduced himself to the family. He said my name is Jim. I will be your driver. Everyone said hi. The driver told everyone to have a seat while he loaded up the limousine. The driver finished loading the limo and got in the vehicle. Dad said thank you for picking us up from the airport.

"It was my pleasure," Jim said.

Jim asked everyone to buckle their seat belts.

Jim drove away from the airport en route to the Hampton Inn. Jim went through a few tunnels and the scenic route. He explained the areas we were about to enter.

"Look at the basketball court. There is a fence around the court. That's odd," Elaine said.

"You will mostly see fenced-in basketball courts depending on the area," Jim said.

"Sometimes, it is for your protection," Jim said.

"Do any of you play basketball?" Jim asked.

"I do," Elaine replied.

"How good are you?" Jim asked.

"I'm OK," Elaine replied.

"What are your plans while you are in New York?" Jim asked.

"We are planning to have fun attending entertainment attractions and shopping," Dad replied.

"If you need any assistance, please allow me to direct you so you will not get lost or frustrated," Jim said.

We finally made it to the hotel.

"Go in and get your keys for the room. I will bring your luggage and take it to your room," Jim said.

Dad and Mom walked in first, and I walked behind them.

Dad and Mom were very impressed with the design of the hotel.

"This is nice," Elaine said.

The receptionist said Hi, my name is Jenny. How can I help you? Do you have reservations?

"Yes, we do," Dad replied.

"The reservation is under Hines," Dad replied.

Jenny gave my Dad and Mom two keys to the room.

Jenny explained the room was on the 2nd floor above the receptionist's desk.

Jenny explained the setup of the hotel. "We have free breakfast, happy hour, fresh cookies, juices, and the exercise room," Jenny said.

Jenny showed us to her left a shelf with various brochures about different attractions in New York.

Jenny also said she would be more than happy to answer any questions we had about the hotel and the attractions offered in New York.

We headed to the room. Dad opened up the door. Our luggage was already in the room. The room was nice, with two queen-sized beds. I asked Dad whether I could sleep in the bed close to the window.

"Yes," Dad said.

I went to the window, and Mom followed me. I was curious about what I could see on the second floor. There was a store across the street, a church, and a lot of traffic. It was a nice view.

"I think we are going to have a nice time in New York," Elaine said.

"We will try our best," Dad said.

"Yes, we will," Mom said.

"Let's organize things in the room and plan to look around the hotel," Mom said.

It took us a few minutes to get things settled. We all finished putting things up at the same time.

Mom suggested we check out the exercise room, eating area, and the business office in case Mom and Dad needed to use the computer.

We found everything with no problem.

"I smell something," Elaine said.

"I do, too," Mom and Dad said.

"What is it?" Elaine said.

"We made some fresh cookies," Jenny replied.

"Where are they?" Elaine asked.

"Look to your left. As you exit the elevator, you will see a stand with cookies and some napkins," Jenny replied.

"You can go in the dining room and get juice or water to drink with your cookies," Jenny said.

"Thanks, we will," they all replied.

We finished eating our cookies and juice. We decided to walk out in front of the hotel to see how it looked outside. We did not see very much while riding in the limousine.

Mom suggested we go across the street to the store. We crossed the road. Mom went to a store with many gift items and purses. A few bags had pictures of people who looked like movie stars. Some bags had a picture of a pretty lady with a background somewhere in Paris. I thought they were cute. Mom bought two purses. I know one was for me; I will allow Mom to pick which one she wants. I was going to take the one she did not select.

We left out of that store and went next door to another store. There was a lot of traffic trying to enter and exit the store. I had to hold on to my Mom's blouse to avoid being lost or left outside the door. That's how fast the people went in and out of the store. The store was more like a grocery store. It reminded me of a one-stop store like H. L. Greens. These kinds of stores have everything you need at reasonable prices.

Mom saw a huddle of people at a table picking, pulling, and throwing things to the side. She got closer to find out what was going on. They had several college T-shirts on sale for $1.00. I told Mom can you get us a few T-shirts?

"Yes, I will try," Mom replied.

My Dad and Mom squeezed in and picked several T-shirts. They found several my size.

"Yeah," Elaine said.

We had enough shopping, so we returned our purchases to the hotel as it was getting late.

"Let's put up our purchases and walk a few blocks to see the town at night," Mom said.

"OK," Dad and Elaine said.

We stepped outside and walked a block to Madison Square Garden. This place has a lot of things going on. I remember something about a boxing event.

There was a lot of traffic in front of Madison Square Garden. I have seen movies about all the traffic in New York. It looked the same, just seeing all the yellow taxi cabs everywhere heading in all directions.

We walked past Madison Square Garden to the next corner. There was a K-mart store. "What? I thought all the K-mart stores were closed. I guess just the ones in Dallas," Mom said.

"I guess not, Mom, because we are about to walk into K-mart," Elaine said.

"Elaine, my Mom used to shop at K-mart when I was younger. It has been over 20 years since I walked into a K-mart store. I love K-mart," Mom said.

Well, Mom, here is your chance to enjoy yourself in K-mart. We only have a short time. The store is about to close," Elaine said.

"I agree we do not have long to shop," Dad said.

"Let's just ride the escalators to the various floors. It will not take long," Mom said.

"Dad, we better watch Mom. She is enjoying herself a little bit too much," Elaine said.

"She is OK. I will make sure she does not get carried away," Dad said.

"See, your Mom did well. She just did as she said. She rode the escalators to the floors, looked around, and we all came to the first floor together before the store closed," Dad said.

"Yeah, good job, Mom," Elaine said.

"Hold your composer, Elaine," Mom said.

"OK, Mom, just kidding," Elaine said.

"Is anybody hungry?" Dad asked.

"I'm hungry," Elaine replied.

Dad and Mom said they were also hungry.

"What does everyone want to eat?" Dad asked.

"Hamburger," Elaine replied.

"I think we have to walk a few blocks to get a hamburger," Dad replied.

I saw a brochure from the hotel about a place called White Castle. They have some excellent hamburgers. "Does everybody feel up to walking a few blocks for a hamburger?" Dad asked.

"No, Dad," Elaine replied.

"Dad, I am about to pass out. I'm so hungry. Is there something closer?" Elaine asked.

"I think I saw a restaurant across the street from K-mart," Mom replied.

"Let's walk a little closer to the restaurant to see if they have pictures on the window of the types of food they serve," Mom said.

"That's a good idea," Dad said.

"I just want to eat," Elaine said.

"Elaine, we are trying to feed you," Mom said.

"OK, Mom," Elaine said.

"OK, Mom, I see the menu. It has plenty to choose from. Let's eat. It looks good to me," Elaine said.

"Slow down, Elaine. Let me or your Dad get behind you to make sure you get the special," Mom said.

"OK, Mom," Elaine said.

Everyone got the special of two or three of their choice for one price.

We carried our food to the hotel.

Dad did not tip Jim earlier today. We saw Jim. He was still at work. Dad's hands were full of the food we got at the restaurant. Dad gave the bag of food to Mom to hold while he got some change out to give Jim a tip. Dad got Jim's attention. He gave Jim $5.00 and told him to forgive him for not tipping him earlier.

"Thanks," Jim said.

"No, thank you," Dad said.

"Good night, everyone," Jim said.

Everyone said good night.

Jim proceeded to exit the front door. It was time for him to leave for the day.

We stopped by the dining room to get something to drink.

"Wait, Dad and Mom. Before we go to the room. Do we have silverware in the bag?" Elaine asked.

"Let me check," No, we forgot to put silverware in the bag," Mom said.

Hold the elevator while I get some. I want to enjoy my food and not pick over it with my fingers," Elaine said.

"Made it just in time. The buzzer was going off as I stepped on the elevator," Elaine said.

Elaine told her Dad second floor, please.

"Watch your step, please next stop, second floor," Dad said.

"You two characters are something else," Mom said.

Well, we made it to the room. Everyone got settled, turned on the television, and started eating.

After everyone finished eating, we all took a bath and got ready for bed.

The next day, everyone got up for breakfast.

We entered the dining room. People were eating at the tables. You serve yourself. Dad found a table. We all got in line to fix our plates.

"Even though I had a nice dinner last night. I'm ready to go for it this morning," Elaine said.

Dad and Mon wanted me to fix my plate first so that I could sit at the table.

I looked at the food first to see if I wanted to eat it. It was OK. I started putting food on my plate.

I saw something in a pan by itself. I asked Dad what it was.

"Hash," Dad replied.

"Hash is the food Curly did not like in The Three Stooges movie," or it was one of them," Elaine said.

"You remember that movie?" Dad asked.

"Yes, if he did not like it, I am not going to try it out today," Elaine replied.

"You do not have to eat anything you might not like," Dad said.

"Get a little portion just in case you do not like it," Dad said.

"OK, Dad," Elaine said.

"I got some eggs, link sausage, biscuit, waffle, potatoes, and orange juice," Elaine said

I sat down at the table. I started eating and shaking my head. Sometimes, when I enjoy myself, I shake my head and close my eyes. It lets me know everything is hunky-dory." "Um, Um, good," as the commercial says on the television advertisement for Campbell Soup.

Mom and Dad came to the table to sit down and eat. They asked me if I liked the food.

I said just awesome.

I did not bother to get seconds because I did not want to be sluggish. But it was tempting. I must watch my figure since I am trying to play basketball at school.

Dad and Mom finished eating their breakfast.

Dad started to read the paper. We waited until Dad finished reading to ask him what was on today's agenda.

Dad finished reading the newspaper and placed it down on the table. He told my Mom and me to wait to leave the table until he returned. He saw the maid. Dad followed the maid to a room behind the dining area. He saw two maids, so he gave them $5.00 a piece.

They said thank you.

Dad went back to the table and said it was time to leave.

"Oh, wait, I forgot my camera in the room," Elaine said.

"I will go with you to the room," Mom said.

Dad waited for them on the first floor near the door.

Mom and I made it downstairs. Dad asked us what we wanted to do.

Mom and I hugged our shoulders and raised our hands.

"Well, let's step out the door and see what direction we will take," Dad said.

"What direction?" Elaine asked.

"Let's walk to the right of the hotel to see what we can see," Dad replied.

Before we got to the street corner, I saw an opening with cars stacked on top of one another.

"Dad, is this a parking lot?" Elaine asked.

"Yes, it is," Dad replied.

"New York has limited space, so they stack the cars," Dad said.

"It looks funny, like the Tonka toys or the trucks that carry cars to the dealership," Elaine said.

We continued to walk to the corner. To the right, we were about to cross the street. There was a small restaurant in the corner of the building.

"Let's cross the street," Dad said.

We crossed the street, walked to the right, and found a perfume store.

That was all Mom needed to know.

We did not have time to open the door. Mom opened the door and walked straight past Dad and me. She walked into the store like lightning. Dad and I stayed near the door. He and I did not have any interest in shopping in that store.

Mom finished shopping. She said she bought a few things. She also said she bought Dad some cologne. Dad said thanks.

"We walked outside the store and looked across the street to the left. We saw a Police station. That's nice to know we have security in the area," Elaine said.

We did not cross the street. We stayed on the same side as the perfume store. We turned left on the side of the perfume store and walked a block until we came to the next street. There was a store on both corners where you could buy gifts. Mom stepped into the store on the left side of the corner. Mom bought some shot glasses, postcards, and a T-shirt. We crossed the street to the right. We came upon a clothes store.

"Let's stop," Dad said.

Dad saw some shirts and jeans at a reasonable price. He also went to the back of the store and found some nice tennis shoes.

"I do not know the last time. I saw my Dad so happy with what he purchased," Elaine said.

Dad was surprised by the cost of the items purchased. He asked the worker whether the store had a website. The worker gave Dad a card with information about accessing the website.

We walked out of the store and continued to walk to the right. I looked inside the store on the corner. This store was calling my name. It had so much I could have spent the night in this store and still not been able to pick something to take home.

"I asked my Dad, could I go in the store to pick something?" Elaine asked.

"Yes, find you a few items, and then come get me so I can pay for them," Dad replied.

"Mom, you want to come in with me?" Elaine replied.

"No, you go in and enjoy yourself," Mom replied.

"I found a few things, like a doll and a small purse. I put them on the counter. I told the merchant I would bring my Dad to pay for my purchase. The merchant said OK," Elaine said.

I went to get Dad. I told Dad I needed him to pay for my purchase. He stopped talking to Mom. Mom followed us into the store. Dad paid for everything.

We left the store.

Walking out the door, we all smelled something that smelled good. We looked around and saw a man cooking on a cart. Dad asked what was on the menu. The man gave us what he usually cooks and how much it costs. Dad said it smelled good, but we recently ate breakfast. Thank you.

We turned around and walked back the same way we came when we got to the corner instead of making a left to return to the hotel. We decided to walk straight another block.

We passed a church. It looked like a church on the other side of the world, not in the United States.

We continued to walk until we came to the corner. It looked like we were walking in a box. The blocks are long. I noticed a Mattel store. I asked my Mom if I could look around in the store.

"Yes," Mom said.

I went into the store. I stayed in the store for a while because I could not determine what I wanted. It took me a bit to make a selection. The next thing I realized, Dad came in and asked, had I made a selection? "No," I replied. Dad said I needed to make a selection. It was time to go back to the hotel.

I selected a necklace. I asked Dad to come in and pay for my purchase. Dad came in and paid for my purchase. Dad asked whether this was all I wanted.

"Yes," I replied.

"OK, everybody, we are heading back to the hotel with our purchases and chill a little while before we find a place to eat for dinner," Dad said.

We sat around, watched TV, talked, and played cards.

"I'm ready to do something different," Elaine said.

"Mom and Dad, are you ready to get out and do something?" Elaine asked.

"Yes," we are Mom and Dad replied.

"I saw a brochure showing a free band playing a few streets over. Anybody wants to go listen," Dad asked.

"Dad, do you know exactly where the band will play?" Elaine asked.

"No, not really, but we can find it," Dad said.

"The brochure said it is close to the Rockefeller Plaza," Dad said.

"That sounds good to me," Mom said.

Everyone started walking several blocks over from the hotel. A lot of people were walking in the exact directions. So we followed them, walked up the stairs, and had a seat. We listened to a few songs and walked over to the Rockefeller Plaza. We noticed the band was already performing by the time we got there. Before we could sit down, good Dad and Mom were already bouncing their heads with the music. They looked like they were enjoying themselves.

The Rockefeller Plaza (Center) has two small buildings surrounded by a tall building. They hold a lot of entertainment in that area. I saw this area on TV or in a movie. Some kids were ice skating in front of the building. There is also a news center in that location.

Dad noticed everyone looked like they were sluggish. Dad said let's call it a night and head back to the hotel. Everyone responded that it sounded good. We started walking back to the hotel. We were so tired when we got to the hotel that we did not stop to get a snack or drink. Dad got in the shower first, then Mom. Mom noticed I was already asleep when she exited the bathroom shower. She did not bother to wake me up.

The following day, we had our breakfast and left the hotel.

Everyone started walking to the left of the hotel toward Madison Square Garden. We walked to the corner behind Madison Square Garden.

I saw an entrance where many people were coming and going fast.

"Dad, what is that place?" Elaine asked.

"That is called Grand Central Station," Dad replied.

"Is that where people can get to where they need to go by riding the train?" Elaine asked.

"Yes," Dad replied.

We stood there a little while to watch the traffic.

We continued to walk a block. The drug store was on one corner, and the Post office was across from the drug store. We are on the opposite end of K-mart.

We crossed the street and saw a White Castle restaurant. We saw so many stores you could shop until you dropped.

We came to a street and made a right. We noticed a movie theater. Dad asked whether we wanted to see a movie.

"Yes," we replied.

After the movie, we stepped outside and noticed a Hello Kitty store. I did not bother to ask Mom if we could cross the street to go shopping.

We continued to walk a few doors down from the theater. There was a store with different things inside, like statues of various movie stars. I took a picture beside Samuel L. Jackson. I thought it was neat.

We walked to the corner where there was a significant shoe store. I am trying to remember the name. As we looked to the left of the street, I asked Dad where we were. "We are at Times Square," Dad said.

Dad, this is a busy place, and it is all lit up but pretty.

"Look across the street. There is a Toy-R-us," Mom said.

Mom asked me whether I wanted to go to Toys-R Us.

"No," I'm good, Elaine said.

I wanted to say for real, Mom. That's the little kid store. But I just smiled after I responded.

"Our daughter is growing up," Mom said.

"Yes, she is," Dad said.

"Dad, this area is in many movies," Elaine said.

"Yes," Dad said.

"Are we ready to?" Dad asked.

"Yes," we replied.

As we looked to the left, we noticed a Red lobster restaurant.

Dad asked if we would like to eat at Red Lobster.

"Yes," we said.

The restaurant was pretty. Mom and Dad ordered their usual. I ordered some popcorn, shrimp, and scampi. We sat by the window.

We left the restaurant to the right when we finished our dinner.

We crossed the street and continued to walk away from Times Square, heading for the hotel.

We were almost at the hotel. We saw a restaurant that had some meat sitting up on a stand.

"Dad, why is that meat on the stand where everyone can see it?" Elaine asked.

"It is a form of advertisement to tempt possible customers to enter the restaurant," Dad replied.

We continued to walk past the restaurant.

We came upon a pastry shop.

"Mom and Dad, could we stop?" Elaine asked.

We went inside, and they had all types of pastry.

Dad selected a slice of cherry pie.

Mom selected a slice of lemon pie.

I selected a slice of pecan pie.

We decided to eat the dessert in the restaurant instead of taking it back to the hotel.

Everything looked so good. I had to sample Dad's and Mom's desserts.

We finished eating and left the pastry shop.

We continued to walk toward the hotel. Everything started looking familiar.

"Yeah, one more block to the hotel," Elaine said.

"Mom looks, there is a Massey store," Elaine said.

"Yes, Elaine, I see the store; it takes up a whole block," Mom said.

Let's continue to walk. It is closed anyway," Dad said.

Dad thought I'm glad it is closed. My wife could spend some change in that store.

"You're right, Dad. It is closed. I bet Mom is also glad it is closed," Elaine said.

"Yes, you know that is my store," Mom said.

"Maybe I will get to shop some other time before we leave," Mom said.

"We shall see," Dad said.

"Look, Elaine, over to your left at the tall building," Dad said.

"What is that building called?" Elaine replied.

"The Empire State Building," Dad replied.

"Are we going to cross the street to tour the Empire State Building?" Elaine asked.

"No, not tonight. I am ready to call it a night," Dad said.

"I agree," Mom said.

"OK," It is sure tall.

"Mom, why are so many people going down in that hole to the left?" Elaine asked.

"Stop pointing, Elaine. I see what you are talking about. That is an entrance to catch the train," Mom said.

"OK," Elaine said.

Many people ride the train instead of the bus or taxicab. Elaine asked.

"Most people in New York would rather ride the train. It is more convenient," Mom replied.

"Mom, where are the train tracks?" Elaine asked.

"They're underground," Mom replied.

"OK," Elaine replied.

"Everybody, we made it to the hotel. Let's get some rest for tomorrow," Dad said.

"OK," everyone replied.

"Wait, Dad, before we go up on the elevator. I need to check to see if there are any cookies left.

"No, all the cookies are gone," Elaine said.

"OK, Dad, you can push the button. I am ready to go to the room," Elaine said.

"Elaine, you just had a slice of pie and a sample portion from my plate and your Dad's. Don't you think you had enough for the night?" Mom asked.

"Mom, you know I like my sweets," Elaine replied.

"OK, don't whisper in my ear when your stomach starts hurting because I did not pack the castor oil," Mom said.

"Mom, I saw the drug store down the street," Elaine said.

"How convenient. That is still no reason to be greedy," Mom said.

"OK, Mom, you are right. I need to watch my eating. I want to make sure I make the basketball team. I need to be able to make those moves and dunk the ball in their eye," Elaine said.

We got on the elevator and went to the room.

Mom asked us whether we wanted to exercise for a few minutes.

"Yes," we replied.

We rode the elevator to the basement. There were only two machines. I let Dad and Mom use the machines first. Dad and Mom finished. I used it for a little while. I was getting sleepy. I wanted to try and beat everybody to the bathroom.

"Dad and Mom, are you ready to go to the room?" Elaine asked.

"Yes," they replied.

We got on the elevator and headed towards the room.

I got to the bathroom first, then Dad, and last Mom.

We all called it a night.

The next day, we got up and had breakfast.

"Dad, where are we going today?" Elaine asked.

"We're going to see the Statute of Liberty," Dad replied.

"The Statute of Liberty," Elaine said.

"Yes, the Statute of Liberty," Dad said.

We left the hotel, rode the train, and caught a boat to tour the Statue of Liberty.

"Elaine, you remember asking questions about people going up and down in a hole? I told you that was where people went to ride the train," Dad said.

"Yes," Elaine said.

"Elaine, we are going down in that hole you asked about to get to the train and then catch a board to tour the Statute of Liberty," Dad said.

"Not sure at this point how for it is," Dad said.

"Let's walk down the stairs to the train. We can ask the person in the information both how to get to the Statute of Liberty," Dad said.

Dad said the attendant provided us with three copies of a map. It will show us various tourist attractions in New York.

"OK, thanks. Let's review the map together," Dad said.

"Where is the Statute of Liberty on this map?" Dad said.

"I found it, Dad," Elaine said.

"I see it on the map. We must ride the Q train, get off, and walk a few blocks to get on a ferry boat. It will take us to the Statute of Liberty," Elaine said.

Dad went to the booth and requested three train passes. The attendant gave Dad the cards and provided instructions on how to use them. The attendant reminded us to ensure the light came on before we proceeded through the entry gate. He said to take our time when we slide the card so everybody can be on the other side together. Watch out; the gate closes fast.

"The train was approaching, and we all got on the together.

We were able to find a long seat for all to be seated.

"Look, Mom, the lady has her dog in a carrying bag on the train," Elaine said.

"Elaine, you know it is impolite to point. Use your inside voice and not talk so loud or point," Mom said.

"The dog is cute. How nice to bring your dog on the train," Elaine said.

"On the wall of the train was an electronic map that showed the directions and train stops on the line and intersections," Dad said.

Dad continued to review the map. He said we should be getting closer to our destination.

The conductor announced over the speaker. The upcoming stop would be for parties who want to tour the Statue of Liberty.

"This is the stop," Dad said.

Mom held my hand before I got off the train to ensure we stayed together.

We walked and saw people walking in the direction to the left. We followed them. The next thing we saw was people dressed like the Statue of Liberty. They were stiff as a rock. They looked real.

I kept looking at them as we passed, and they did not move.

There were booths with various souvenirs, drinks, and snacks.

There was a ticket booth to the right of us where you could purchase tickets to ride the boat to see the Statue of Liberty. It was a long line.

Dad got in line and purchased the tickets.

We got in line to ride the boat to see the Statue of Liberty. There was a long line. As soon as we got close, the attendant closed the entrance and said it was at capacity. We had to wait for the next boarding.

"I'm sure it will not take long," Dad said.

"Mom, you see her?" Elaine asked.

"Yes," Mom replied.

We started boarding the ferry boat. "Everyone, let's walk to the top," Dad said.

The ferry boat pulled away from the bank, heading toward the Statute of Liberty.

"We arrived at our destination," Mom said.

People were waiting to board as we were exiting the ferry boat.

As we were viewing, souvenir tables were set up with a tent and without a tent.

We walked around to where we could view the Statue of Liberty. She looked so real. It was a pretty sight to see.

Dad asked if we wanted to go up inside the Statue of Liberty.

"No," we replied.

"Well, I will see you when I return," Dad said.

It was not windy, so I was allowed to view it from the top of the Statue of Liberty.

Mom saw a viewing machine near the walkway.

"Mom, what is that?" Elaine asked.

You can place money in the machine and view things long distances.

"May I try?" Elaine asked.

"It makes things look closer," Elaine said.

"Yes, it does," Mom said.

"Mom, you want to see before the time runs out? Elaine asked.

"Hurry up," Elaine said.

"OK," Mom said.

"I see things like they are so close, I can touch them. But I know better," Mom said.

"Wow, Mom, this is all some," Elaine said.

Dad finally came down and shared his experience of what he saw.

"It is like living on top of the world. There is no other experience than what I just experienced, and it was great," Dad said.

"You can see New York closer from on top and the five boroughs for miles and miles," Dad said.

"You ladies, OK?" Dad asked.

"Yes, we're fine," they both replied.

We walked around a little and then returned to the ferry boat to leave.

The ferry boat was now docking so we could leave. We waited a few minutes for more passengers.

When we got on the ferry boat, we went to the top for a better view of New York City.

The driver announced we would stop at Ellis Island before heading to the main dock.

"Dad, why are we making a stop?" Elaine asked.

"Probably to educate us why there is an Ellis Island. From what I know about the place, it was the check-in point for all immigrants entering the United States. You will see when we dock," Dad said.

"OH," Elaine said.

We arrived at Ellis Island. Everyone walked into the building. There were pictures of immigrants who came to America with their children and family. You can see they carried all their belongings, such as luggage and other items of value, with them on the trip to America.

"This is very educational," Elaine said.

We walked around just looking at things on the wall and enjoying being a part of history.

The building has several rooms for various historical exhibits. They were fascinating exhibits.

We walked to the back toward the bathrooms and restaurants.

We saw a machine that can print your ancestry genealogy.

A lady was talking to us. She said she found out information about her great-grandfather. She was able to print the information and take it home. She even called her family and told them what she had learned about her great-grandfather's history. The lady was so excited and about to cry because of the information she had found. She said her mother had been telling her the history of the family. For years, her mother has been telling her the family's history. She felt sad that it took her this long to believe what they had been saying about the family's history.

She can't wait to see the expression on her family's faces with the proof she found.

Dad and Mom thought the lady shared an exciting story with some strangers.

"We can understand where she is coming from," Dad and Mom said.

We entered our family's last name, and nothing came up.

We continued to walk to the back, where everyone was eating. The restaurants had anything you wanted to eat.

We were not hungry, so we walked around.

We headed back to the entrance to dock the boat and leave.

We got on the ferryboat and returned to where we came on board.

"Riding on the board is a sight," Elaine said.

I would encourage anyone to take a trip at least once to see the Statute of Liberty," Dad said.

"I agree," Mom said.

We made it to the dock, and everyone got off the boat.

We walked several blocks, following the crowd to the train.

Dad knew if he came one way on the train, we needed to go back the opposite to return close to the hotel.

We got on the train. There was only standing room. We walked to another car and found seats.

Dad paid attention again to the map in his hands and on the wall of the train.

Since we are already on the train, we can ride a few blocks from the hotel to walk down Canal Street.

"Canal Street is where there are a lot of places to eat and shop," Dad said.

"OK," Mom said.

We got off the train at the Canal Street exit. We walked up the stairs onto the street.

There were people, traffic, and stores. It was a busy street.

"There are different areas you can go to get what you need, such as purses, shoes, seafood, and eat at various restaurants," Dad said.

We walked several blocks just viewing what the owners were selling.

Some people would approach you and ask whether you want to buy different things.

Mom wanted nothing because she was saving money to shop at Massey near the hotel.

Dad did not see anything of interest.

Walking, we saw a small restaurant hidden behind one of the stores.

"Let's go in and have something to eat," Dad said.

We went in and had a seat. The waiter gave us a menu.

Dad asked for the combination Lo mien.

Mom asked for the same thing.

I ordered spaghetti.

The waiter brought some noodle chips to snack on until our meals were ready.

It took a few minutes, and they brought all our meals.

I was hungry. I did not realize I was smacking on the chip until Mom told me to slow down and not be so noisy.

"Sorry, Mom, that entire sightseeing and walking made me hungry," Elaine said.

We finished eating and read our fortune cookie.

Dad opened his. "It said you will have a future endeavor on your job in a few months," Dad said.

"Do you know something that you have not shared with me?" Mom asked.

"Yes, I was trying to hold off until I was sure I wanted the job," Dad said.

"Can you share it now?" Mom asked.

"My boss wants me to fill the recently available management position. I told him I would give him an answer when I come back from vacation," Dad said.

"Are you going to accept the job?" Mom asked.

"Yes, as soon as I get back home. I will give my boss a call," Dad said.

"Wonderful, I am proud of you," Mom said.

"I am proud of you too, Dad," Elaine said.

"Now, Elaine, it is your time," Dad said.

"OK," Elaine said.

My cookie says you have taken steps to do group things at school. An action in your favor will await you," Elaine said.

"Mom, that means I can play basketball at school. I cannot wait to talk to the coach to see when practice starts," Elaine said.

"We are both happy for you, Elaine," Mom said.

"Mom, you are next," Elaine said.

"OK," Mom said.

"It says doors will open for you to spread your wings to other interests," Mom said.

"What does that mean?" Dad asked.

"I have been thinking about applying for another position in the school district," Mom replied.

"What do you want to do?" Dad asked.

"I want to work in the office or maybe at another school," Mom replied.

"How long have you been considering changing your career?" Dad asked.

"For several months, I have been thinking about doing something different. Do not get me wrong. I love my job. I have not had any problems. I want to do something different," Mom replied.

"Just take your time. Do not be in a hurry to take anything," Dad said.

"No, I know better than to apply for anything that comes up. I have plenty of time to review the job description and see what best fits my skills," Mom said.

"We are in your corner whatever you decide to do," Dad said.

"Since everyone has shared what was in their fortune cookie. It is getting late. We need to catch the train to the hotel," Dad said.

They left a tip and headed out the door to the train station.

"Do you remember the exit?" Elaine asked.

"Why do you think I stayed on one side of the street? So we would not get lost and could find our way back. Your Dad is not a dummy," Dad replied.

"I know, Dad, you are smart," Elaine said.

"Everybody, let us go down this exit. We need to go down and go back in the opposite direction," Dad said.

"OK, you lead the way," Mom said.

Mom whispered in Elaine's ear. What would we do if your Dad was not with us?

"We would be walking around like a chicken with our head cut off even though we had a map," Elaine replied.

"I agree we would be up the creek," Mom said.

"It's almost time for us to get off the train," Elaine said.

"You are right. I'm surprised you paid attention, Elaine," Dad said.

"Yes, sir, I am paying attention," Elaine said.

"This is our stop. Watch your step. Let's walk upstairs to the street level. We should come out right where we entered," Dad said.

"Dad, here we are, one block from the hotel," Mom replied.

"Let's cross the street. I'm ready to dive in the bed," Elaine said.

"No, young lady, you know the rules. You have to take a bath first before you lie in bed. We have been gone all day. You know good and well you are a little tangy," Mom said.

"I know, Mom, just testing you," Elaine said.

"Sure you are, young lady," Mom said.

"Serious, Mom, I was going to bathe before I got in bed," Elaine said.

"Enough said. I am heading to the bathroom to bathe," Elaine said.

"OK," Mom said.

Elaine only stayed in the bathroom briefly. Everybody was ready to bathe and go to bed.

"Good morning. I hope everyone had a good night's rest. Let's clean up and have breakfast," Dad said.

Everyone got ready, left the room, and walked to the elevator, heading downstairs to each breakfast.

As the family got off the elevator, Jenny got their attention.

Jenny said you do not worry about going to get breakfast. I made a tote bag of breakfast items for you. I knew you wanted to get out on the town. So everything is in the sack bag: Coffee for Mom and Dad, Orange juice for Elaine, Breakfast burritos, Sugar, Cream, and napkins.

"Thanks, you thought of everything," Dad said.

"Yes, thanks," Mom and Elaine said.

They headed out the door of the hotel.

"I'm not sure what we are going to do today. Anybody has any suggestions?" Dad asked.

"The Museum," Elaine said.

"Everyone agrees to tour the Museum?" Dad asked.

"Yes," Mom and Elaine replied.

"OK, I need to go upstairs and get my map," Dad said.

"That's OK, I brought mine," Mom said.

"Great," Dad said.

"Mom, we are making all the arrangements to tour the museum. We need to eat our breakfast before it gets cold," Elaine said.

"We can eat and drink what we have as we walk to the train," Dad said.

"True," Mom and Elaine said.

"OK, we finished with breakfast. Let's get on the Q train and transfer to another train. It will take us straight to the museum entrance," Dad said.

We followed the map's directions and listened to the train conductor. We got off the Q train. A sign above us showed the train we needed to ride to the museum. We just had to wait for it to come by. It finally arrived, and we got on. The conductor said the next stop would be the museum.

We all walked in and paid our entry fee. The attendant gave us some brochures. We got out of the way and started reading where we wanted to start our museum tour.

We walked in from the back into a large area of the museum.

"Mom, look, I have seen some of these exhibits in a movie. I'm not sure the name of the movie," Elaine said.

"Are you sure?" Mom asked.

"Yes, Mom, I would not be pulling your leg. I watched the movie several times. Everything came alive at night in the museum," Elaine said.

"OK, if you say so," Mom said.

"We saw giant prehistoric animals. They looked so real," Elaine said.

"This is a huge Museum. It has historical exhibits and educational things to see on several floors. It will take several days to view everything in the museum," Mom said.

"Where do we start?" Mom asked.

"We can always start anywhere. We will still end up on the first floor," Dad said.

"Mom, it does not matter where we start," Elaine said.

"Elaine, make sure you stay close. This place is so huge you could get lost," Mom said.

"You are right, Mom. I will ensure I stay close to you and Dad," Elaine said.

"We will start on the first floor and work our way up," Dad said.

We walked in and out of the floor room to view the exhibits.

"It is incredible how the historic exhibits look so real it is almost scary," Elaine said.

"We will walk in this area. Elaine, make sure you stay close. I know you do not want me to treat you like a toddler and hold your hand," Mom said.

"No, Mom, please allow me to respect what you have told me to do and not worry about me walking away from you and Dad," Elaine said.

"Dad and Mom, look at the man on the horse. Will he come alive?" Elaine asked.

"NO, He will not come alive," Dad and Mom said.

"OK," Elaine said.

"Mom, look at the exhibits in that window," Elaine said.

"What window are you talking about," Mom asked.

"The window over there with the cowboys and Indians," Elaine said.

"OK, I see it," Mom said.

"Oh, they look like real people, just smaller in size," Mom said.

"You said you saw some of the exhibits in a movie, but you do not remember the movie's name," Mom said.

"Yes, Mom," Elaine said.

"What happened in the movie?" Mom asked.

"The museum came to life after hours. Everything could talk, walk, and run. They took the night watchman through a lot after hours, but he eventually adjusted. It was a nice movie. Sorry, I do not remember the movie's name," Elaine said.

"That's OK," Dad said.

"Mom, can I hold your hand for a little while? It is creepy now, knowing that I saw a few exhibits in the museum that came to life in the movie. I would not want to be around after hours in the museum," Elaine said.

"We will not be able to see all the exhibits anyway, Elaine. We have plans to visit other places before returning to the hotel," Dad said.

"OK," Elaine said.

"Mom, let's go in this direction," Elaine said.

"OK, you lead the way," Mom said.

"Mother dear, look at what is behind the glass," Elaine said.

"I see an Eskimo exhibit. Is there anything wrong with what you see?" Mom asked.

"Mom, listen to me, read my lips, whispering and pointing. This exhibit was also in the movie," Elaine said.

"OK, Elaine, seeing things or objects that look familiar is alright. That does not mean they are going to come to life. Calm down. Nothing in this museum will harm you," Mom said.

"Elaine, it is possible that someone could have used a few exhibits from the museum in various movies. Did you enjoy the movie?" Mom asked.

"Yes, I never thought I would see them in real life in a museum," Elaine said.

"Look at it like this. You might be the only person out of a handful who remembers the story and what happens in the movie. So count it all joy to relate that you saw the movie and the exhibits are real in the movie," Mom said.

"You understand? So what you saw in the movie should help you to picture what the director was trying to portray," Mom said.

"Yes, Mom, I understand. Wait till I get back home. O boy, do I have a story to share with my friends," Elaine said.

"Mom, can we find Dad and head back to the hotel or go to the next place on the agenda," Elaine said.

"What about the other floors?" Mom asked.

"I've seen enough, and very educational," Elaine said.

"I think Dad is in the area across the hall," Mom said.

"Hey, Dad, are you ready to leave?" Elaine asked.

"I'm ready if both of you are," Dad replied.

"We are ready to leave," they both said.

"May I have a souvenir?" Elaine asked.

"Sure, what would you like?" Mom asked.

"Can you see if they have a dinosaur, Indian, or Pocahontas?" Elaine asked.

"Dad, you can get it for me," Elaine asked.

"OK," Dad said.

Mom and I stood around the tall statue with the man sitting on the horse. I dare not say anything else. He was also in the movie.

Dad finally made it back.

He bought me a chain with all the characters.

"Thanks, Dad," Elaine said.

"Are we going to walk or take the train?" Dad asked.

"We do not care. Either way is fine with us," Mom replied.

"Let's walk toward Central Park," Dad said.

"You know the direction we should be walking, Dad?" Elaine asked.

"Yes, follow me. I got this," Dad said.

"Central Park, see you did not believe me," Dad said.

"Well, we made it so far good," Mom said.

"It is beautiful," Elaine said.

"Is this where people come to play and enjoy themselves with their families?" Elaine asked.

"Yes," Dad replied.

"We can walk on the sidewalk and look at the nice scenery," Dad said.

"Look over there in front of the restaurant. Someone was very creative. The bushes or hedges look like animal shapes. How neat they are all around the restaurant," Mom said.

"Elaine, I'm like you. I also remember seeing the same bushes and hedges around a restaurant in a movie. It may have been in more than one movie," Mom said.

"It just slipped my mind the name of the movies. I remember two great actors who played separate roles in the two movies," Mom said.

"That's OK, Mom. At least I'm not by myself in remembering what I have seen. Thank you for being on home plate with me. It made me feel a little better. I'm not the only one half remembering things seen," Elaine said.

"Dad, we've seen enough of Central Park. Where do we go to catch the train to the hotel?" Elaine asked.

"Let's walk one more block to see if we are close," Dad said.

"Here we go. Let's get on the train and return to the hotel," Dad said.

"Everyone got on the train heading to the hotel.

Elaine mentioned she was hungry.

"We all are hungry," Mom said.

"We will get something to eat as we get closer to the hotel," Dad said.

"Let's get something to eat across the street from K-Mart. There is another place on the same side of the hotel across the street from Madison Square Garden. So what will it be?" Dad asked.

"The one across the street from K-mart is closer to the train station," Dad said.

"It does not matter to me. All I know is my stomach is talking to me. I'm getting hungrier and hungrier, and we are still on the train talking about food," Elaine said.

"We almost there, Elaine," Dad said.

"We just needed to determine where to eat so we would know what stop to get off on," Dad said.

They got off the train and walked to the restaurant across from K-Mart.

They selected their meal and prepared their take-out tray to go.

They returned to the hotel around the corner up the street.

Everyone got on the elevator and headed to the room.

They entered the room, had a seat, and started eating their meal.

Dad asked if there were any other places they would like to go before they called it a night.

"When I finish eating. I want to do something else," Elaine said.

Dad placed his food tray on the nightstand to check the brochure on current attractions in New York.

"The Lion King and Drum Beat are in town. He wanted to know which one they would like to attend. He needed to order the tickets for the attraction?" Dad asked.

They asked Dad to make reservations for Drumbeat.

"It starts at 8:00 p.m.," Dad said.

"We can make it," Mom said.

"Dad made the reservations.

Elaine was trying to stay awake. She started working on her Sudoku book.

Around 7:00 p.m., Dad said let's get ready to leave. If there is a long line, it is best to get there early. Also, we will go now because we must walk past Times Square to get to our location.

They made it to the show on time. They had everyone come in and sit anywhere they saw a drum. That means you will have to pick the drum up to sit down. Place the drum on the floor in front of your seat.

The performance was outstanding; everyone had to participate in beating the drums as instructed.

Dad had no problem playing the drums. He played drums in school.

They provided good instructions on when to hit the drums. I was able to keep up. I did not look to see if Dad or Mom was keeping up. I was trying to keep up with the rhythm.

The show was over. Mom could see my face that I enjoyed the show.

We walked back to the hotel and got ready for bed.

Tomorrow, we will leave the hotel around noon to the airport to take a flight back to Dallas.

Mom did not have time to shop at Macy's. That's OK. She can shop when she gets home.

The next day, we woke up early to have breakfast and pack.

Dad told the Bellman we needed transportation from the hotel to the airport. We wanted to leave around 12:30 p.m. The flight departure time from La Guardia to Dallas was 2:30 p.m.,

The Bellman came to our room at noon to get the luggage. We already had everything packed before he arrived.

We got ready to leave the room. Dad left a few dollars on the bed for the maid.

Dad checked out of the hotel via express checkout. We had to leave the card at the front counter and get in the limo.

The receptionist said bye and have a safe trip back home. She also said she hoped we'd come again.

Elaine remembered Dad tipped everybody else but the receptionist. She reached into her purse and pulled out her little coin purse. It had three dollars folded together. Elaine walked to the receptionist and said thank you for all your help.

"Thank you," The receptionist said.

"That was very generous of you," Dad said.

"It sure was," Mom said.

We got in the limo and rode to the airport.

We arrived before time to the airport. The Bellman placed our luggage on the walkway. Dad gave the Bellman a tip.

"Thank you, the Bellman said.

We checked in and got our boarding passes. We walked to the terminal where we would have a seat and waited to board the plane to go home.

"The plane is here," Dad said.

The Stewardess announced the flight to Dallas would be boarding in 30 minutes.

We got on the plane road economy style in front of the plane.

The plane landed, and we walked to baggage claims to get our luggage.

We picked up our luggage.

Dad called to see if a park-and-ride shuttle bus was in the area to take us to our car.

The park-and-ride shuttle bus was only five to ten minutes away.

We got on the shuttle bus, which took us to the park and ride parking lot. We carried our luggage to the car.

We put the luggage in the trunk and drove home.

We arrived home, and my friend Lucy was waiting on the porch for me as we drove up. She helped get the luggage out of the trunk.

"Make sure you put up your things before entertaining Lucy," Mom said.

"OK, Mom," Elaine said.

"Lucy, you can come into my room while I put up my belongings," Elaine said.

"OK," Lucy said.

"Did you enjoy yourself, Elaine?" Lucy asked.

"Yes, I did," Elaine replied.

"One day, I will give you more information about what we did while we were in New York. I'm trying to put everything up and relax," Elaine said.

"I know you're busy. I thought I would help you and then go back home," Lucy said.

"I'm going to let you finish what you are doing. I will see you in the morning for school," Lucy said.

"OK, bye, Lucy," Elaine said.

Elaine finished putting up everything.

She went to her parents to let them know how she enjoyed herself on the trip.

"Dad and Mom had already put up their things. They were in the den drinking coffee. I told them I enjoyed the trip. It was an experience I'll never forget," Elaine said.

"Where glad you enjoyed yourself," Dad and Mom said.

"I'm going to ask next time we take a trip if Lucy can come with us," Elaine said.

I'm going to ask Dad and Mom now if that is possible.

"Dad, Mom, do you think we could include Lucy on the next trip?" Elaine asked.

"We would have to ask her parents in advance. We will not be going on another trip for a little while. But it will be around the same time we went on this last trip," Dad said.

"I agree we have to plan our trip. We have things at home that might interfere with the timing," Mom said.

"OK, I understand," Elaine said.

Elaine gave Lucy a call since she had put everything up.

"What have you been doing while I was on vacation?" Elaine asked.

"Road, my bike, went to the gym, played basketball, went to the movies, attended a birthday party, went camping, and played house with my doll Lucia," Lucy replied.

"Wow, you did a lot," Elaine said.

"I called you to let you know the next time we go on a trip, you are more than welcome to come, as long as your parents approve it," Elaine said.

"That would be awesome," Lucy said.

"By the way, I bought you a souvenir. I will bring it to school and give it to you during lunch tomorrow," Elaine said.

"Thanks. See you in the morning," Lucy said.

DEE AND THE BABYSITTER

THIS STORY IS ABOUT A family the parents decide to take a vacation and leave the kids at home.

The Brandon family has two children, Dee and Ciara. Dee is ten, and Ciara is 17.

Dee attends Franklin Grace Elementary, and Ciara attends Amber High School.

The schools are a block, a part with trees, and a lake that separates the schools. You cannot see the school from the trees. Some students have made a trail between the woods to get to the other school.

Dee and Ciara are good students. They get good grades, and both are teachers' pets. They get along with the students at school. They like playing sports such as basketball, football, and bike riding.

The two of them do so well in school; at home, their parents reward them with a weekly allowance.

Dee has a best friend that lives several blocks from him. His name is Duce. They hang out often and do different things together, like buddies. They both call each other brothers.

Ciara is maturing and set in her ways. She is growing up and does not hang out with many friends at school. The only close friend Cara has; her name is Paris. She knows Paris is bossy, but she doesn't care. She goes along to get along. Paris is still her best friend regardless of how she might treat her. They both talk to each other about anything, and it will stay between the two of them.

Sometimes Paris will spend the weekend with Ciara.

I stay away from my sister and do not bother her when she has company. I don't want to embarrass her around her friend.

It's OK. Ciara asks me to help her do something when her friend visits, like go to the kitchen and get both of them a drink and a snack.

I know how teenagers are. They're some bossy girls. It does not hurt me to entertain them for a little while. I know how far to go. I'm always saying something to my parents about the situation. I know what to do if it ever gets to that point. They never ask me to do anything too offensive. So I do it for my big sister.

Paris and I are pretty close. If I scratch her back, she will scratch mine if needed.

My sister does not have any interest in boys. She is more of a tomboy. She likes doing things boys do.

When my sister hears rumors about parties held at school, she is not interested. But, if there is a sock cop, all ears are open who's attending the dance. Ciara likes to dance. Paris will always meet Ciara at the school so both can attend together. Both girls want to do the line dance. They like to be on the first row when the music begins for the line dance.

When Paris comes to visit, she likes to talk to me. She always asks me what

I've been doing. I would always respond the same as usual. She would ask me how I was doing in school. I would reply fine. I would tell her I make good grades.

"Do you give the teachers any problems?" Paris asked.

"No," Dee answered.

"Do they have a dress code at your school?" Paris asked.

"No," they do not have an address code. I can wear whatever I want to wear," Dee answered.

"Are you going to do anything special today?" Paris asked.

"Not sure at this point. Duce, my friend might call me to do something or maybe not," Dee answered.

When Paris gets to asking questions, look out. She doesn't want to stop. Paris is friendly and talks a lot but does not mean any harm. She is the only child at home. She probably gets lonely.

Paris is my sister's best friend, and she is mine as well. She treats me friendly, and I treat her the same.

"Mom, can Paris spend the weekend?" Ciara asked.

"Yes," Mom replied.

"Good, I want to have a little fun this weekend," Ciara said.

"Remember, you and your company must clean up and not be loud. Don't forget you are not the only ones who live in the house," Mom said.

"OK, I will watch it," Ciara said.

Ciara could not wait until the weekend. She had planned on sharing something personal with Paris. She was unsure how Paris would react but would share it with her this weekend.

Ciara called Paris and asked what was up for the weekend?

"Nothing," Paris said.

"Would you like to hang out with me this weekend?" Ciara asked.

"Let me ask my mother, hold on," Paris said.

"Mom, may I spend the weekend with Ciara?" Paris asked.

"Of course, as long as you promise me you will be responsible and help clean up and do other things as needed while you are there," Ciara's Mom said.

Paris came back to the phone. It's OK. "Mom approved me spending the weekend," Paris said.

"Good. What time would you be over tomorrow after school?" Ciara asked.

"Around 6:00 P.M.," Paris answered.

"OK, that is a good time," Ciara said.

"I will see you at school tomorrow and when you come over," Ciara said.

"OK, bye," Paris said.

The next day everyone went to school.

Paris made it over to the house around 6:15 P.M.

She knocked on the door.

"Someone is at the door," Mom said.

"OH, it is probably Paris," Ciara said.

"Dee, will you open the door," Ciara asked.

Paris came in and spoke to everyone. They both went to Ciara's room.

"Dinner will be ready in 30 minutes," Mom said.

"Dinner is ready," Mom said.

Everyone came to the table to eat. Dad said grace.

We ate our dinner. Everyone was quiet at the table.

We finished dinner.

Ciara and Paris cleaned the table and the kitchen.

We all sat in the den and watched television. My parents wanted to watch westerns. Ciara and I do not care for watching westerns. So most of the time, we went to our rooms. But since we had company, we sat briefly instead of leaving the table and heading to the room.

We eventually got up and said good night to our parents.

"You do not have to rush off to your rooms," Dad said.

"We are not. I'm full as a tick and ready to lay it down. You do not want to see us fall asleep on the couch. That would not be very pleasant for you to wake us up and we have company. Besides, this is quality time for you and Mom," Ciara said.

"You trying to say Western is not your type of entertainment? Dad replied.

"Dad, you know I'm a teen, and I'm not alone in what I'm about to say. Westerns are OK for you and Mom. But, if the movie has nothing to do with rapping, singing, or love scenes, it does not keep our attention," Ciara said.

"OK, our kids are growing up. I hope I'll be around to explain that there is more to life than the interests you just shared," Dad said.

"Leave them alone. The understanding of the children changes all the time regardless of how you teach them family morals and what makes sense. They have to learn for themselves," Mom said.

"Let them go in their rooms. You are missing the good part of the movie correcting the children this time of night," Mom said.

Everyone went to their rooms.

When I got to my room, I thought I had been waiting to hear from my friend Duce for a few days. So I gave him a call. As usual, he is busy or not at home. The line just rang, no answer.   I hung up without leaving a message. I will see him at school Monday.

I guess. I will read a few pages in the "Skunky" story from "Cindy and Jane" book. My Granny is the author of this book. I need to read more, so when she asks me out of the blue, have I taken the time to read any stories? I will have an answer. She keeps saying we must be interested in reading some of the stories before she leaves this earth. That way, if we have any questions, she can answer before she is no longer around to answer. I finished reading the story. It's funny how the animals in the story kept active by doing fun things like people and being mindful of others. Now, I can talk with my Granny about the story, and she would know I read it.

I do not hear any noise in the other room. Ciara and Paris are probably asleep. Since I'm still up, I will play a few games on my play station. Next thing I knew. I fell asleep with the remote controller in my hand.

I got up the following day and went to the bathroom. Mom saw me on my way to my room.

"Dee, you left the PlayStation and light on again. I turned them off," Mom said.

"Thanks, Mom," Dee said.

Mom made breakfast and asked everyone to get up and get ready to eat.

Dee was the first to come into the kitchen.

"What plans do you and Dad have for the weekend?" Dee asked.

"I'm not sure right now. Give me a few minutes. I will get with your Dad," Mom said.

"OK," Dee said.

"Choose what you would like to eat for breakfast. Eggs, bacon, sausage, and toast are on the stove. There is cereal and milk on the table. There is orange juice in the refrigerator," Mom said.

Everyone finished eating, and the kids cleaned the kitchen.

Dee went outside to play a few hoops of basketball in the backyard. Two hours later, Dee's Mom called him into the house.

Mom and Dad asked us to come into the den. They would like to speak to everyone.

"What's going on? We hardly have meetings," Ciara said.

"I agree," Dee said.

Paris turned to look at Ciara and Dee. She did not know what to say since she was visiting. She did not know what to do, so she stood behind Ciara and Dee.

"Have a seat," Mom and Dad said.

We all sat down, including Paris.

Dad announced their anniversary is today, and they plan to get away this weekend.

"Who will keep us while both of you are away?" Dee asked.

"I think all three of you are old enough to stay home alone," Mom answered.

"I agree," Dad said.

"Your Dad and I are looking forward to getting away and spending time together," Mom said.

"We hope all three of you will be on your best behavior in our absence. Do not answer the door. No one should leave the house. No more company is allowed while we are gone, just Paris. Is this understood?" Mom asked.

"Yes," they all replied.

"Does anyone have any questions?" Dad asked.

"I do," Dee said.

"Mom and Dad, you have never left us by ourselves. I'm not sure if it is a good idea," Dee said.

"My sister is the babysitter?" Dee asked.

"Dee, you will be OK. You think your sister will treat you differently by us not being here?" Mom asked.

"I don't know, Mom," Dee said.

"Dee, you will do just fine," Mom said.

"OK, both of you have a nice time while we sit here wondering if both of you are OK," Dee said.

"Come here Dee. We will be back tomorrow. I promise you. Nothing is going to happen to us," Mom said.

Mom hugged Dee to comfort him in thinking everything would be OK.

"OK, everyone, we need to pack. We will be leaving in a few hours. We will leave the hotel information on the front table, or you can call us on our cell phone. Plenty of food is in the refrigerator and pantry. No need to cook anything. In the kitchen there is plenty of bottled water and drinks," Mom said.

"If anything happens life-threatening do not hesitate to call.   We will check on all of you to make sure everything is OK," Mom said.

"Now, any questions?" Mom asked.

"Speak now are far ever hold your peace," Mom said.

No one had any more questions.

Mom and Dad finished packing for their trip.

The next thing we saw was Mom and Dad with their luggage at the door.

"Bye, everyone we are heading out the door," Dad and Mom said.

"Bye," the kids replied.

Ciara and Paris went to the room.

Dee locked the door and also went to his room.

"Someone was ringing the doorbell. Dee peeped out the window and saw it was the pizza man. Dee called his parents to see if it was OK to open the door. Dad answered the phone.

"Is it OK to open the door for the pizza man?" Dee asked.

"We ordered pizza for all of you. You have a choice between pepperoni, sausage and combination ham with pineapples. The tip is on the table. Open the door for the pizza man," Dad said.

Dee got the money off the table and hurried to the door. He opened the door and apologized for the delay. He was getting the tip. Dee received the pizzas. He gave the pizza man a tip and said thank you.

"Thank you," The pizza man said.

Dee closed the door and placed the pizzas in the oven.

"Girl's the pizza has arrived," Dee said.

"Who bought pizza?" Ciara and Paris asked.

"Mom and Dad," Dee said.

"I put the pizzas in the oven until we get ready to eat," Dee said.

"Good idea," Ciara and Paris said.

"Dee, want to play Monopoly?" Paris asked.

"Yes," Dee said.

Ciara won.

They all decided to play Dominos.

Dee won.

The last game played was Trouble.

Paris won.

Mom and Dad called to check on us. We told them everything was OK. They said they would see us tomorrow.

We finished playing games and decided to eat pizza and watch television in the living room.

"Paris, what would you like to watch?" Ciara asked.

Paris selected the Black Panther.

"Everybody is talking about that movie. That's a good selection. I've been meaning to watch that movie," Ciara said.

Everyone was into the movie. No one was talking. When the movie ended, everyone commented about the film and said. It was good.

"Now, it's clearer why several kids at school during recess talked about the characters in the movie and shared their views, asking them if they had seen the film," Ciara said.

"Thank you for selecting the movie Paris," Ciara said.

Everybody went to the kitchen for seconds on pizzas.

Everybody helped clean the kitchen, said good night, and went to bed.

The next morning would be the day Mom and Dad return home.

Dee got up first and went to the kitchen. He ate cereal, then returned to his room to clean and wash up. Dee did everything he knew to do so he had some time to read another story from his Granny's second book, "Joey and London." The first story in the book was about Joey and London. They liked to do daring things outside, like exploring the unknown. The two boys had no idea what lurked in the woods but were willing to explore. They did not allow anyone to know what happened in the woods. It was a secret between the two of them. Both boys experienced fear, and they were able to overcome and work through it.

I will eventually tell my Granny I read two stories from her books. She would love for me to share what I read, and that I took the time to read her books.

The girls were still in the room. I knocked on the door and told them to clean up before Mom and Dad came home.

"Get away from the door," Ciara said.

"OK, you know what Mom said," Dee said.

"I know what she said," Ciara said.

"You do not know when they will be home, so Paris and I can lay around a little bit longer," Ciara said.

"If you say so," Dee said.

"He might be right. Let's get up and do what we need to do. We can always come back and lay around," Paris said.

"OH, behold the two bursts of sunshine decided to come out of the room," Dee said.

"Shut up Dee," Ciara said.

"Just kidding," Dee said.

"I already bathed and had my breakfast. Now I'm ready to see Mom and Dad," Dee said.

"Don't worry. Dad and Mom will be back home sometime today," Ciara said.

Dee went back to his room to play on his PlayStation.

The girls cleaned up and came in the kitchen. Both of them pulled out a breakfast sausage on a stick from the freezer. They warmed it up in the microwave and sat down at the table to eat. Both girls cleaned up after themselves and headed back to the room.

"I heard some noise at the door. I peeped out the window. It was Dad and Mom. They're here," Dee said.

I opened the door someone else was with them.

"Granny," Dee said.

Everybody hugged Granny.

"Kids introduce your friend to Granny," Dad said.

"Granny, this is my best friend Paris," Ciara said.

"Hi, Paris I'm the kids grandmother. You can call me Granny," Granny said.

"OK, it is a pleasure to meet you," Paris said.

"Likewise," Granny said.

Dad and Mom said they happened to be in the area and decided to stop by Granny's house, so she chose to stay with us for a week or two.

"Dee, get me a drink of water. No ice in a glass," Granny asked.

"Dee, when you finish getting Granny some water go to the car and get the rest of her stuff," Mom said.

"Granny will sleep in the spare room, so bring her things in and put them in the spare room," Mom said.

Granny finished drinking her water and gave the glass back to Dee,"

"Thank you," Granny said.

"You welcome," Dee said.

Dee returned the glass to the kitchen, washed it out, and placed it in the strainer in the sink.

Dee went to the car to get Granny's belongings. He placed them in the spare room.

Granny went to the living room and had a seat.

"Dee turned on the television," Granny asked.

Dee turned the television on.

"Granny what do you want to look at?" Dee asked.

"I would like to watch the channel that has Western Movies," Granny said.

"OK, that's good," Granny said.

"Is there anything else," Dee asked.

"Go get the box out of the trunk of the car," Dad asked.

Dee brought the box from the car and asked where he should put it.

"Ask your Granny," Dad said.

"Bring it to me," Granny said.

Granny started taking things out of the box.

"What is in the roaster pan?" Dee asked.

"Teacakes," Granny said.

"Oh my God, feast time," Dee said.

Dee could not wait to see what else Granny had in the bag.

Granny pulled out coffee, bacon, molasses, a pound cake, and a berry pie.

"I know we are going to pig out Granny can cook," Ciara said.

"Granny, you brought a lot," Dee said.

"Yes," Granny said.

"Where are my greens and cornbread?" Granny asked.

"Did anyone get the bag out of the trunk?" Granny asked.

"I saw the bag, but Granny told me to get the box, and that is what I brought," Dee said.

"Would you go get the rest of the food?" Granny asked.

"OK," Dee said.

Dee went to the car and got the rest of the food.

Dee brought the food in and gave it to Granny.

"Is there a place in the refrigerator to put the food?" Granny asked.

"Yes," let me help you Mom with the groceries," Mom said.

Mom put the items in the refrigerator for Granny.

"Thanks," Granny said.

Everyone went back to the den and had a seat.

The time was getting late. Paris Mom called for her to come home.

Paris got her stuff together and said goodbye to everyone.

"Baby give Granny a hug before you go," Granny said.

Paris came over to Granny and hugged her.

"Granny I hope to see you soon. Enjoyed your visit," Paris said.

"Baby, you stay sweet. I'll see you next time," Granny said.

"OK," Paris said.

Ciara walked Paris outside and watched her go into her house before she went back into her house.

Dee went to the kitchen to get some water before he went to bed.

Granny was still up looking at the television.

"Granny said who is it?" It is me Granny Dee.

"What are you doing?" Granny asked.

"I'm getting ready for school," Dee said.

"Come here," Granny asked.

"OK," Dee said.

"Come sit by me. I will not hold you long," Granny asked.

"OK," Dee said.

"Have you had time to read any stories in my books?" Granny asked.

"Yes," Dee said.

"I read a story from the book called "Cindy and Jane" "Skunky" and a story from "Joey and London" "Joey and London," Dee said.

"What did you like about the stories?" Granny asked.

"In the story "Skunky." It was interesting to read about animals doing things of interest just like people. In the story "Jane and London." The two boys are friends. They are exploring the woods, but they both make it through. The boys showed they cared for one another and helped each other out during trouble. The boys shared a secret that only the two of them knew what happened in the woods," Dee said.

"Dee in the story "Skunky." All the animals were friends and liked to play baseball. They all loved one another, but sometimes Skunky would let off a terrible smell, and he could not help it. They devised an idea to help Skunky with his smell, and it worked. He felt bad, but they all went through a test together and came out alive. That's what friends are about helping one another out in the time of trouble," Granny said.

"Dee in the story "Joey and London." Sometimes secrets should not be told and then other times an adult need to know what happened. Joey and London determined that if they told anyone, all sorts of things could have happened to the cub and its family. Sometimes decisions are made for the benefit of all parties involved. When you get into situations, you determine the right thing to do. You understand?" Granny asked.

"Yes," Dee said.

"OK, give me a hug before you go to bed," Granny said.

Dee gave his Granny a kiss and hug. He told her good night.

"Good night see you in the morning," Granny said.

THE WISHING TREE

THIS STORY IS ABOUT A young girl spending summer vacation with her grandparents for the first time.

Grace is 8 years old, and she loves being away from the city to spend time with her grandparents.

Grace heard her grandmother say she would ride to town and get a few items from the feed and grocery store.

Grace loves to go to town because she would get a few lickerish sticks from the jar on the stand near the cash register.

Grace likes to talk to Mr. Waits at the feed store.

Grace's grandmother Mrs. Fellows, asked Grace did she want to go to town?

"Yes," Grace replied.

Grace brought her socko toy with her because sometimes it can take a little time for Granny to get everything she needs from town.

Grace put on her shoes to get ready for town.

Grace's Granny said, "Come on."

Grace said, "I am ready."

Grace's grandfather, Mr. Fellows, worked in the field, so he was not aware of us going to town.

Grace decided to leave her grandfather a note letting him know they were gone to town. Grace left the message on the kitchen table.

When granny drives, she likes to tell stories of places she used to go that no longer stand. Things she did when she was young.

Grace would listen and also ask questions.

Grace's Granny remembered so many things. She also remembered people's names.

Granny started telling me who I was kin to. I knew I would never be able to remember all those names as she could.

It takes about 15 minutes to get to town from my Granny's house.

When Granny gets to talking, the time goes by fast. We would be there before you know it.

Granny stopped at the feed store first and then at the grocery store.

Mr. Waits was looking at us as we approached the feed store entrance. We both said, "Hi, Mr. Waits'.

"Hello," Mr. Waits' replied.

He asked my Granny if she wanted the usual.

"Yes," she replied.

"Do you want me to put it on the account?" Mr. Waits' asked.

"Yes," she replied.

"Do you want me to put everything in the truck?" Mr. Waits' asked.

"Yes," she replied.

Mr. Waits finished putting everything in the truck.

We told Mr. Waits, "Bye," and thank you. We will see you next month.

As we were driving by, Mr. Waits said to tell Mr. Fellows to stop by.

"Ok," Granny replied.

My Granny drove around the corner to the grocery store.

Granny picked up a few items: can goods, syrup, jam, peanut butter, flour, sugar, meal, milk, salt, bacon powder, washing powder, bacon, sausage, margarine, cooking grease, peppermint sticks, days work, and soap.

Granny finished grocery shopping. We went to check out.

Granny saw Mr. Lindsey, her neighbor standing in line waiting to check out in front of us. She asked him how he was feeling.

"Much better," Mr. Lindsey replied.

He told my Granny thank you for dinner last Sunday.

"You are welcome," Granny replied.

Mr. Lindsey asked Granny, "Who was the little girl with her? Granny said she was my granddaughter. We call her Grace.

"Hi, Grace, it is a pleasure to meet you," Mr. Lindsey said.

"Likewise," Grace replied.

"I've some peaches, cabbage, and watermelons you can have from my farm," Mr. Lindsey said.

I might have some plums and berries for your granddaughter, little Ms. Grace, Mr. Lindsey said.

"Thanks, we will be over sometime next week," Granny said.

"I look forward to seeing you next week," Mr. Lindsey said.

The cashier checked us out.

"Wait; let me take your groceries to the truck. I'm buying just a few items. Just give me a minute I will help you," Mr. Lindsey said.

Mr. Lindsey paid for his groceries and pushed the shopping cart outside to the truck.

He put everything in the truck and said is that it?

"Yes," Granny said.

"Ok," bye Mr. Lindsey said.

"Bye," Granny said.

Mr. Lindsey lives alone. Granny said he has always given people things and asked people to come by to visit him.

"Let's go next door and look at some clothing," Granny said.

When we came out of the grocery store, I thought granny was ready to leave town and return home.

I saw a beautiful purple dress in the window as we approached the clothing store. I dared not ask Granny to buy the dress since she had already spent a lot on feed and groceries.

I walked behind Granny in the store. She asked me whether I would like something out of the store. She said she had enough money to purchase the item.

I asked Granny, was she sure she had enough money? "Sure, I have enough pick out what you want," Granny said.

Grace picked out the purple dress in the window. "She asked the clerk, did they have a size 8?"

The clerk said, "She did not have any smaller sizes."

Grace's smile turned to a frown. Her granny saw that she was unhappy about not being able to get the dress because the store was out of stock for her size 8.

Grace's Granny asked the clerk to please look in the back to see if maybe there was a size 8 in stock.

The clerk was in the back a pretty good while. She finally came from the back with something in her hand. It was a purple dress. She did find her size.

Grace was so happy that she would be able to purchase and wear the dress. Grace told the clerk, "Thank you for going the extra mile to look for the dress."

The clerk said the dress was $10.00.

"Good, that is about what I've left after grocery shopping and the feed store," Granny said.

The clerk wrapped the dress in brown paper and wrapped a string around it to be easy to carry.

Grace asked her Granny "Was she going to buy herself anything?"

"No," not this time, maybe next time, Granny replied.

"Thank you," Grace and her granny left the store and walked to the truck.

Granny had gotten everything that was on her list.

Granny drove the long way back home. There was something she wanted to show me.

Grace did not remember going in the direction her granny was taking her.

Granny took us down a dark road with nothing but trees. We got to the end of the road. I saw a lake, a large brown and green tree with limbs leaning over on the side of the tree.

"Granny this is not the way we go home," Grace said.

"I'm taking a different route, Granny said.

"Why," Grace asked.

"I want to show you The Wishing Tree," Granny said.

"What is so important about The Wishing Tree?" Grace asked.

"Why do you call it The Wishing Tree?" Grace asked.

"The tree has a lot of history behind it for our town. The tree has been standing for centuries. People have had meetings and parties around the tree. The town believes the tree represent goodness. At night, the tree glows. We are not sure if it is a reflection from the moon and the lake, but it actually glows. Everybody believes that it is a unique tree. People pray around the tree. Some call it a miracle tree. Others say if you are seeking answers in your life take it to the tree," Granny said.

Granny told me a story about when she went to the tree. She prayed for something to happen in her life. It is believed that prayer changes things. She has seen this happen after people came to pray around the tree.

"Granny what was your reason for visiting the tree?" Grace asked.

"In case you did not know Grandpa was sick last year. So it was time for me to use my faith and not just hear people's reason for visiting the tree. I made a visit to the tree. I opened up my heart and left it there at the tree believing your Grandpa would be healed. In a week your Grandpa was doing things around

The Wonders of Life And All That It Holds

the house like he never was sick. I'm a believer. I was so happy his condition had turned around for the better," Grandma said.

"Ok, I understand," Grace said.

"I want to share what I know about the Tree in case you have a desire to visit the tree, "Granny said.

"The information shared with you about The Wishing Tree should be shared and never die," Granny said.

"The knowledge about the tree is part of our family heritage and town secret," Granny said.

"Thank you, Granny in sharing the information about the town secret," Grace said.

"I'll always remember the story about The Wishing Tree," Grace said.

Granny and Grace walked back to the truck and drove home.

Grandpa was waiting for us, looking out the front screen door.

"Did you get everything we needed from town?"Grandpa asked.

"Yes, we did," Grandma said.

Grandpa went to the truck and unloaded everything.

He put the groceries in the house on the table. He left the things from the feed store on the porch.

"How was the trip to town?" Grandpa asked.

"It was an experience," Grace said.

Grace got to meet Mr. Waits at the feed store. He was kind and helpful. "He said tell you to come to see him," Granny said.

"Ok, Thank you for relaying the message," Grandpa said.

"What else happened in town?" Grandpa asked.

"I got to meet Mr. Lindsey. Granny said he had been sick, but he looked well in the store," Grace said.

"That is true. We did see Mr. Lindsey as he was checking out at the grocery store. He looked so well compared to a week or two ago. Mr. Lindsey said he had some vegetables and fruits for us. We could pick it up at any time. Granny said we are going over to his house next week to pick up the items," Grace said.

"You are supposed to be leaving to go home Saturday," Grandpa said.

"Could I stay one more week so I can visit Mr. Lindsey's farm?" Grace asked.

"Ok," Grandpa and Grandma agreed to let Grace stay an extra week.

"Thanks," Grace said.

Grace and her granny started putting up the groceries. Cleaned the kitchen and got things ready for supper.

After supper, Granny and Grace cleaned the kitchen and went out on the porch to sit on the swing. Grace saw a truck coming up the road. Granny said it was Mr. Lindsey. Mr. Lindsey came up and said he brought the items he mentioned in the grocery store.

"You did not have to do that. We would come next week," Granny said.

"No bother, I was coming this way anyway to bring Grace a gift," Mr. Lindsey said.

"I'm feeling much better, and I want to give Grace these items before they go bad," Mr. Lindsey said.

"I'm coming tomorrow to help you Mr. Lindsey, with things that need to be done on the farm," Grandpa said.

"Thank you so much. I need some help every now and then. My strength is not what it used to be," Mr. Lindsey said.

"No problem, I'm more than willing to help," Grandpa said.

Mr. Lindsey gave me the things he promised in the store. The plums and berries looked so eatable.

Granny told me to put my fruit in the refrigerator and come back outside since we had company.

Grace did what her granny asked her to do.

Grace stepped outside on the porch, and Mr. Lindsey gave her a black box. She was so amazed at what could be inside the box. Grace opened the box and saw 8 silver dollars. She also saw a clear bag like a sandwich bag. She could see through the bag, and she immediately knew where it came from. The bag had a small branch and leaves from The Wishing Tree.

"Grace you know what you have in your hands?" Mr. Lindsey asked.

"Yes," I know what it is and where it came from," Grace replied.

"Thank you," Grace said.

"I'll cherish the items you gave me," Grace said.

Grace gave her grandma and grandpa a kiss and a big hug. She said this summer has been the best summer ever. She said she looked forward to visiting The Wishing Tree next summer."

GRETA AND DIANE FIND A HOBBY

THIS STORY IS ABOUT A young girl by the name of Greta.

Greta is a relatively simple young lady who has plans to attend college.

She attends Greenfield High School in Boot County. She is a junior in the 11th grade.

She likes helping her Mom around the house and doing girly things.

She is trying to follow in her Mom's footsteps by attending college and receiving a master's degree. She is excited to finish high school and attend college. She is not sure what her educational field will be.

Greta likes jogging with her Mom in the evening after school. She also enjoys going to the gym and exercising with her Mom. They both always stop at the smoothie shop before they go home. Then, they go to the park, sit, drink their smoothie, and watch the ducks. Greta loves animals, and she enjoys feeding the ducks. The park has food you can buy and feed the ducks. It is only ten cents.

Greta's Mom always prepares dinner before going to exercise. She prepares a large bowl of Caesar salad. They usually drink water or have another smoothie already in a pitcher.

Greta follows her Mom's lead, believing that drinking plenty of fluids and eating healthy foods is essential.

Both of them finished eating.

Mom cleaned the kitchen, and we relaxed in the living room.

Mom, I have homework and a paper that is due tomorrow. I'm heading to my room to finish up.

My paper is due tomorrow. I have homework and am heading to the room to finish it.

The next day, I went to school.

Mom went to work. She works in the administrative office across the street from the school.

We usually ride together since the school is across the street from her office.

We live four blocks from the school and Mom's job. Suppose something is going on at school. I would call Mom to let her know the reason for staying after school. Knowing someone's whereabouts is for safety reasons. It is essential to inform Mom when something is out of the norm.

Today, Diane and I are staying after school to help the gym teacher set things up for the Sock Hop tomorrow morning. We already have it approved by our parents. It will be before school starts around 7:00 a.m.

The gym teacher, Mr. Dawns, likes having Diane and I do things for him because he knows we will do it right.

Mr. Dawns wants the first dance of the year to be lovely since the PTA recently approved a dance at the school.

Mr. Dawns wants Diane and me to ensure the speaker system works. He wants us to test the system. He asked us what music would be appropriate to play at the dance.

He wants us to do a trial run of his available music. He needs to know if he should purchase more music. He also would like pictures on the wall and a few chairs.

He knows the janitor will make sure the floors are clean, as well as the bathrooms.

Mr. Dawns asked us who would play the music and accept the money.

"I will sit at the door and collect the money," Diane said.

"I will play the music," Greta said.

"OK, we have that out of the way," Diane said.

"Let us go to the art room and get some colorful art paper," Greta said.

"OK," Diane said.

"Mr. Dawns, we are going to the art room for some posting material. The door is still open. We do not need a key," Greta said.

"Do not forget the other things that need to be taken care of," Mr. Dawns said.

"OK, they both replied.

Greta and Diane walked to the art room. They picked up some colorful construction paper, two poster boards, markers, glitter, glue, ruler, and tape.

"How about we go to the teacher's workroom and get some large colored paper," Diane said.

"Good idea," Greta said.

Greta and Diane were able to get into the teacher's workroom. They rolled all the paper so it would be easy to carry. They decided to pull three yards of brown, red, blue, and yellow.

They walked back to the gym.

They told Mr. Dawns their back.

"OK," Mr. Dawns said.

"Did you find everything you needed?" Mr. Dawns asked.

"Yes," they both responded.

"Let us take everything to the table," Diane said.

"OK," Greta said.

"Let us start with the small stuff first. We need two posters as follows:

One poster board will be posted on the wall close to the table where the money will be received before you can enter into the Sock Hop.

The second poster board will be placed on the wall across from the gym door.

Both poster boards should include the cost to enter the Sock Hop and a few creative decorations and pictures.

"Please note on the poster boards that there will not be in and out access. You can work on the poster boards," Greta said.

"OK," Diane said.

"If anything is unclear, please ask questions, and I will clarify," Greta said.

"I will start working on the banners for the walls. When you finish the poster boards. You can help me with the banners," Greta said.

Diane finished both poster boards and taped them to the door and wall as instructed.

Diane entered the gym to help Greta with the banners.

"I finished my task. Now I'm ready to help you with the banners," Diane said.

"Let's draw pictures on the first colored banner to go on the wall. Then, go to the next color, and so on. We will come together at one point and tape it on the wall," Greta said.

"We can figure out what wording to write on the banners as we go along," Dianne said.

"Yes, let me put this banner down. Be right there," Greta said.

"Here, let us place them on each gym wall where everyone can see. Now stand back, Diane, and see if it is positioned right. See how the pictures are and the writing?" Greta asked.

"Yes, I can see everything on the banner," Diane said.

"Now, let us put the other banners on the other walls," Greta said.

"Yes, we did a good job," Greta said.

"Now we need a table on the side where the door is open so the people can pay and then come in the gym," Diane said.

"Girls, do not worry about a table. We will have one by tomorrow," Mr. Dawns said.

"OK," they both replied.

"We need a chair," Diane said.

"It is getting late. We need to hurry up," Greta said.

"So true," Diane said.

"I will go on one end of the banner, and you go on the other. Be creative, draw whatever; I will do the same," Greta said.

"I am going to cut some people out of construction paper and paste it on my blue banner," Diane said.

"I am also going to draw some records, music, and signs a little creativity," Grace Diane said.

"It is five o'clock," Diane said.

"Our goal is to finish by six o'clock," Greta said.

"Yes, let us try for six o'clock," Diane said.

"OK," Diane said.

"OK, done," Greta said.

"Yes, done," Diane said.

"I am also going to do something creative. Write Sock Hop in bold letters. Trace the foot on the banner with glitter. Yeah, we finished. It is 5:45 p.m.," Greta said.

"Are you finished?" Mr. Dawns asked.

"Yes," we both replied.

"We have all the banners on the wall readable from a distance," Diane said.

"Clean up so we can go home," Mr. Dawns said.

We cleaned up and left the lights on for the janitor. We left out the exit door near the girl's bathroom.

We walked with Mr. Dawns to his truck.

We sat in the back cab of the truck. Mr. Dawns sat in the front seat.

Mr. Dawns dropped Diane off first, and I was last.

"I told Mr. Dawns thank you for bringing us home. We will see him tomorrow morning at the Sock Hop," Greta said.

"OK," Mr. Dawns said.

Greta walked into the house. Her Mom asked if everything was OK and ready for the Sock Hop?

"Yes. The gym looks nice," Greta said.

"OK, do not forget to do your homework," Mom said.

"I finished my homework during study hall at school," Greta said.

"Wonderful, that is my girl," Mom said.

"Mom, I am going to go in my room to get ready for school," Greta said.

"Are you going to take a bath?" Mom asked.

"No, I will take care of that in the morning," Greta said.

"OK, get some rest. Good night," Mom said.

"OK, see you in the morning," Greta said.

The following day, Greta got up and did her regular preparation for school. She noticed Mom was not ready. She knocked on Mom's door.

"I am almost ready," Mom said.

Mom was a little slow this morning getting it together for work. Wonder why? She was looking for something she could not find. I guess she found it because she said I found it.

I'm not sure of the complete delay this morning. Sometimes, it is better to leave well enough alone before getting scolded for trying to help.

Also, when trying to help adults with things. They pretend to not need your help.

I waited in the living room and turned on the television. I turned on Mr. Peppermint and Mr. Kangaroo until Mom was ready to leave.

Mom was ready. "Let's go," She said.

We headed out the door and got in the car.

We saw Mr. Hunt walking his dog as we exited the driveway.

We waved in passing.

We finally made it to school. Mom continued to drive to work.

Diane was waiting at the front door of the school.

"I approached her and asked, was she ready for the dance?" Greta asked.

"Yes," Diane answered.

The girls walked a little way to the gym. They heard music playing before they got to the door.

They saw bright lights all over the gym as they approached the door.

"Look, did we do this?" Diane asked.

"No, Mr. Dawns went to the store and bought a few things for the dance," Greta said.

"Mr. Dawns met us at the door.

"Good morning. Let us get things ready. We have five minutes," Mr. Dawns said.

"OK," they both responded.

Mr. Dawns had the table in place and a box on the table to collect the money.

He went to the store and bought some more music. He knew what to buy to impress the students, faculty, and staff.

Mr. Dawns hopes this will be a lovely dance so the word can get out. Moreover, possibly other events will be held at the school.

Dean and Bobby were the first to pay and come to the gym. After they came in, others followed.

"Looks like more kids are starting to come in," Diane said.

The kids finally started dancing after Grace and Andy got on the floor.

"I am going to change it up a little bit and play some music the kids like to hear," Greta said.

After Greta changed it, more people began to get on the floor.

It was getting close to time to go to class.

The kids started leaving the gym 5 minutes before the bell rang. An announcement was made that everyone should prepare to leave for class in five minutes. We asked the kids to pick up around them as they left out the door.

We could hear the kids talking as they exited the gym that they enjoyed the event.

Diane and Greta cleaned up and started walking out the door when Mr. Dawns caught their attention.

"Thank you for both of your help. The dance was a success," Mr. Dawns said.

"Thank you," Diane and Greta said.

Diane and Greta walked to class. They went in opposite directions when they left the gym.

All day everybody was talking about the dance. They talked about it in the morning announcements. Mr. Dawns spoke a little about the event. He was so happy with how it turned out. Mr. Lake, the principal, gave a speech after Mr. Dawns. He congratulated the students on their behavior and would let them know when another dance would be available at the school. He was thinking maybe around Valentine's or Thanksgiving.

"Good Job, Vikings," Mr. Lake said.

Greta saw Diane at lunch. They usually like to sit by themselves. Judy, Travis, and Jane followed them to the table. The kids saw them assisting at the dance and thought they would chat with them during lunch.

Greta and Diane said hello to everyone. They were wondering how they happened to be following them and sitting at their table today.

Travis was the only boy. He asked if they would like to participate in a surprise birthday party for his Mom. She thinks she is going to a school meeting at the Recreation Center. He will share the details later.

"What do you think?" Travis asked.

Diane and Greta walked from the table to the corner near the exit, going to the playground. They talked it over. Both knew they could not make a final decision until they got approval from their parents.

"Can we let you know this evening after school?" They both asked.

"Yes, here is my cell phone number. Call me with your answer," Travis said.

"Great, I will be looking forward to your call," Travis said.

"Hope the opportunity is as good as it sounds," Diane said.

"Well, it sounds good to me. We can get exposure to the town on our talents in party preparations and entertainment," Greta said.

"We will have people talking about us who never bothered to speak," Diane said.

"Do you still want to do it?" Greta asked.

"Yes, I would not miss it for the world," Diane said.

"OK, we do not want to spend our whole lunch on this subject," Greta said.

Diane and Greta went back to class. They met after school and said a few words. They proceeded off the school grounds to go home.

Greta reminded Diane to get with her parents. She would give her a call after she spoke with her Mom.

"OK," Diane said.

Greta continued to walk across the street to her Mom's job. Her Mom was tidying things up to leave for the day. Greta sat in the front and waited for her to come and tell her to let her go home.

Mom was ready, and we left out the door.

"How was your day?" Mom asked.

"It was fine," Greta said.

"I am not sure about your response, young lady," Mom said.

"Is there something on your mind?" Mom asked.

"Mom, we do not have to talk about it right now?" Greta asked.

"No, you can talk about it when you get ready," Mom said.

"Thanks, Mom," Greta said.

Mom drove the car into the driveway.

"Hello," Mrs. Liza, the neighbor, said.

We said hello and continued to walk into the house.

Greta walked to the kitchen to get a drink of water.

Mom walked to the den, turned on the television, and had a seat.

After drinking her water, Greta went into the den to sit with her Mom.

Now is an excellent time to ask permission to attend Travis's event at the Recreation Center. Diane will call any minute now with her information if she can attend the event. The next question would be if I can hear the event.

"Mom, a friend at school is having a special event at the recreation center on Saturday. He wants Diane and me to help him out," Greta said.

"Sure, you can help your friend out with his event. I knew something was going on. It is hard to fool Mom," Mom said.

"Good. I will call Diane to see if everything is OK with her parents," Greta said.

The doorbell rang.

"Mom, are you expecting company?" Greta asked.

"No, are you?" Mom asked.

"No, not that I know of," Greta answered.

"Well, go see who is at the door," Mom said.

Greta opened the door. It was Diane.

"I could not wait until you called me, so I came over to tell you my parents said it is OK to attend the event," Diane said.

"Who's at the door, Greta?" Mom asked.

"It is Diane," Greta said.

"Tell her to come in," Mom said.

Diane walked to the den.

"Hi, Ms. Williams," Diane said.

"Hi, did you come over to talk about what you and Greta will be doing Saturday?" Mom asked.

"Yes," Diane replied.

"The both of you must be very excited," Greta's Mom said.

"Yes," they both responded.

"Well, girls, you can continue to talk about your Saturday event. There are many things to do around the house. Ladies, go ahead and make plans for the event," Mom said.

"Do you have any idea what you will wear on Saturday?" Greta asked.

"I thought about wearing my ripped jeans," Diane responded.

"Girl, wake up and smell the coffee. No, you cannot dress around older people at that party. What type of blouse? Do not say a tank top," Diane said.

"Well," Greta said.

"Precious, do you want us to get fired at the door?" Diane asked.

"I am trying to picture in my mind what to wear. Just want to be comfortable," Greta replied.

"Check this out. We serve the community, so we must dress for the occasion," Diane said.

"Yes," Greta said.

"No way will both of us dress like a pretty mess, and someone whispering about how unprofessional we dressed for the occasion," Diane said.

"Diane, I know a little how you think. We are best friends," Greta said.

"Yep, you are right. We are best friends," Diane said.

"Well, why don't we wear jeans, no holes, and a T-shirt or nice blouse," Greta said.

"OK," Diane said.

"Mom and I are going to the movies and having dinner in a little bit. Come with us," Greta said.

"Thanks. I have a report to work on and have not figured out what I want to write about," Diane said.

"When is it due?" Greta asked.

"Wednesday," Diane answered.

"I can help you Sunday with your report," Greta said.

"Would you?" Diane asked.

"Yes, I would do that for my friend," Greta said.

"OK, I will call my Mom right now and see if I can hang out with you guys," Diane said.

The phone rang. Mom picked up and asked why Diane was calling.

Diane asked her Mom if she could attend an outing with Greta and her Mom.

"May I speak with Ms. Williams?" Diane's Mom asked.

"OK, hold on," Diane said.

"Greta, my Mom wants to talk to your Mom," Diane said.

Greta took Diane's phone to the back, allowing both Moms to talk.

Mom was in the washroom folding clothes. Greta gave her Mom Diane's phone because she was asked to by Diane's Mom.

"Greta, why are you giving me this phone," Greta's Mom asked.

"Mrs. Brown wants to talk to you about Diane attending the gathering this evening," Greta said.

"Is there something I need to know before I get on the phone with Diane's Mom?" Greta's Mom asked.

"No, I think she wants to verify what is going on," Greta said.

"Hello, Mrs. Brown. Diane would like to attend an outing this evening with me and Greta. She wants permission to do so," Greta's Mom said.

"I want to confirm Diane's information about you and Greta's outing this evening," Diane's Mom said.

"Yes, no problem. Diane can tag along, so Greta will have her best friend with her for the evening," Greta's Mom said.

"Hold on, Mrs. Brown, the girls are trying to get my attention. What is it?" Greta's Mom replied.

"Mom, I have Diane's fare. I can pay it with the money saved from allowance," Greta said.

"OK, I am back. Greta said she would pay everything for Diane," Greta's Mom said.

"Well, wonderful, but if you need me to pay you back, no problem," Mrs. Brown said.

"We will drop her off after everything is over," Greta's Mom said.

"OK, that will work. Enjoy," Mrs. Brown said.

Greta's Mom gave the phone back to Greta to give to Diane.

"Ladies, where will we eat, and what movie will we watch?" Greta's Mom asked.

"How about we see King Kong 2 at the movies and eat at Chili's?" Greta suggested.

"OK," everyone replied.

"Hold up. Let me put this last load of clothes in the washer," Greta's Mom said.

Mom came back from the washroom and asked if we were ready.

"Yes, we are ready," they both said.

"Let us get in the car," Greta's Mom said.

"Greta pulls the front door tight to make sure it is closed," Greta's Mom said.

"OK, Mom," Greta said.

"Greta, did you check to see what times the movie will be playing?" Greta's Mom asked.

"Mom, I completely forgot to check," Greta said.

"Go ahead and check if we have to wait a while. We might as well go eat first," Greta's Mom said.

"Checking now," Greta said.

"I got it. The next time the movie will play will be at seven. It is now six thirty," Greta said.

"We can make it. Hope there is no long line," Greta's Mom said.

"We are here. It does not look like a long line," Diane said.

"You are correct, Diane. There is no long line," Greta's Mom said.

"Let us get in line, ladies," Greta's Mom said.

"Mom, you are not in line. It is over here," Greta said.

"Sorry it has been a while since I have been to the movies," Greta's Mom said.

Greta got in line first to pay for her and Diane's ticket in the movie. In all the excitement, she left her purse on the bed in her room. "Mom, I left my purse on the bed," Greta said.

"No problem," Mom said.

Mom walked up to the counter and paid for everybody's ticket. We walked inside the building to watch King Kong 2.

"Anybody wants a snack or thirsty?" Greta's Mom asked.

"No, Mom, we will eat after the movies," Greta said.

"Mom, did you bring a sweater?" Greta asked.

"Yes, I brought two sweaters just in case it gets cool while watching the movie," Greta's Mom said.

"We sat up front. We better sit further back in the middle. Come to think of it. King Kong can get pretty loud," Greta said.

"I already know," Diane said.

We happened to find three seats close together.

Mom likes to sit at the end of the row.

We found our seats just in time. The advertisements had just started, and the lights were turned down low.

We watched the whole movie. We jumped a few times but all made it through the film.

When the movie was over, we walked out the door.

"How did you ladies like the movie?" Mom asked.

"It was scary but good," Diane said.

"It was good," Greta said.

"Well, I also enjoyed the movie," Diane's Mom said.

"Let's continue to walk out of the movie theater to eat," Greta's Mom said.

We got in the car and drove for about 15 minutes.

We entered the Chili's parking lot. We parked and walked into the restaurant. The hostess asked how many were in our party.

"Three," Greta's Mom said.

"Follow me, please," The hostess said.

"Where would you like to be seated?" the hostess asked.

"Mom, where would you like to sit?" Greta asked.

"May we have window seats?" Mom asked.

"Yes," the hostess replied.

"Your server will be at your table in a few minutes," The hostess said.

The waitress came to the table and said her name was Nancy. She said she would be our server. She wanted to know whether we wanted to order something to drink.

We all ordered lemonade.

The waitress came back with our drinks. She asked if we were ready to order our meal?

Mom ordered first. She wanted a pasta salad.

Greta ordered second from the three-pick menu.

Diane was unsure what to order, so she requested the same meal Greta had ordered.

The server brought our food.

They looked at their meal as the waitress placed them on the table.

Nancy, the server, asked if there was anything else we needed.

"No," Mom said.

"Ladies, we have been served. Who will say grace?" Mom asked.

"I will say grace," Diane said.

"Lord, thank you for this food we are about to receive in Jesus' name," Diane said.

Everyone said Amen and started eating.

We started talking about school and college.

We finished our meal and left a tip on the table. We walked out of the restaurant.

Nancy, the hostess, said goodbye and came again.

"OK," we replied.

We walked to the car. Greta realized she had left her sweater on the table. Greta got out of the car and went back to the table. The sweater slid on the floor. Greta picked it up, and she saw the hostess coming toward her. She asked if everything was OK.

"Yes, we lost a sweater, but we found it, "Greta said.

"Good, I'm glad you found it," the waitress said.

Greta and Diane walked back to the car.

"We found the sweater, Mom," Greta and Diane said.

"Great," Mom said.

We left the restaurant and headed toward Diane's residence.

"Mom did not know where Diane lived. It was not far from the house. We gave her directions. When coming from a different direction, it is not very clear. Diane, are we going in the right direction?" Greta asked.

"Yes, my house is to the right on the corner," Diane said.

Mom drove into the driveway.

"OK, we enjoyed you," Mom said.

"Yes, Diane, we must do this again," Greta said.

OK, Diane got out of the car and walked to the door.

"See you tomorrow at the Recreation Center," Diane said.

Mrs. Brown opened the door for Diane.

Mrs. Brown waved and said thanks.

Mom drove out of the driveway and headed home.

Greta and her Mom made it home. Mom drove the car into the driveway.

When Greta got in the house, she thanked her Mom for the outing and for allowing Diane to join them.

"Good night, Mom," Greta said.

"Good night. See you in the morning," Mom said.

Mom stayed up a little while and watched television.

Mom finally went to bed.

Greta got up Saturday morning and ate breakfast. She also cleaned the kitchen and her room. She noticed her Mom was still asleep.

Greta called and asked what time did she want to leave?

"You and I can walk to the recreation center around 11:30 a.m.," Diane said.

Mom said she would take us to the Recreation Center so we would not have to walk. She is still asleep," Greta said.

"That is OK. Mom already said she did not mind dropping us off," Diane said.

"Wonderful," Greta said.

"OK, we will see you in a few," Diane said.

"Good Morning," Mom said.

"Oh, you up?" Greta asked.

"Are you ready for me to drive you girls to the Recreation Center?" Mom asked.

"Mom, since you were still asleep, Mrs. Brown volunteered to take Diane and me to the Recreation Center," Greta said.

"Oh, I am sorry I slept a little longer than I thought," Mom said.

"Diane and her Mom are on their way," Greta said.

"Was that a car blowing the horn?" That is probably them," Mom said.

"It could be Diane and her Mom," Greta asked.

Greta opens the door. It was Diane. She wanted to know if I was ready?

"Yes, I am ready," Greta said.

"Mom, Diane, and her Mom are here to pick me up," Greta said.

"OK, have a good time," Mom said.

Greta walked out the door to get in the car.

"Greta, before you get in the car, would you have your Mom come to the door," Diane's Mom asked.

"Yes, Ma'am," Greta said.

"Mom, Diane's Mom wants to speak with you," Greta said.

"I am not presentable," Greta's Mom said.

"Mom, they could care less what type of clothing you wear," Greta said.

"That is right. OK," Mom said.

Mom walked to the car.

"Hi," I just wanted you to know I appreciate you are allowing Diane to hang with you and Greta yesterday. I'm returning the favor by taking the girls to the Recreation Center," Diane's Mom said.

"Thanks," Greta's Mom said.

"Bye, it was nice talking to you," Greta's Mom said.

"Girls enjoy," Greta's Mom said.

They drove off, heading toward the Recreation Center.

Diane's Mom told the girls it is essential to be well-behaved while away from home. People tend to blame parents when they see how kids react in public. People will think you do not have good home training. It would be best to behave well in public and away from home. Do not disappoint your family, and use good judgment and nothing less.

"Do both of you understand?" Diane's Mom asked.

"Yes," they both replied.

Diane's Mom dropped the girls in front of the Recreation Center. "She told them to have a nice time," Diane's Mom said.

Greta and Diane entered the building.

Travis was waiting for them at the door.

"Welcome," Travis said.

"We are glad to be here," they both replied.

"OK, ladies, here are the party's decorations, supplies, music, and food. Set it up nicely," Travis said.

"Diane, what do we need to do first?" Greta asked.

"Put up the decorations on the wall and tables, etc.," Diane said.

"OK," Greta said.

"The decorations we have to work with are simple. We do not have to be creative as we did in the gym for the Sock Hop," Greta said.

"Here, Diane, you take these pictures and tape them on the wall to the left. Tape the rest to the wall on the right. We have to watch our time," Greta said.

"OK," Diane said.

"I finished my decoration," Greta said.

"I also finished my decorations," Diane said.

"What is next?" Diane asked.

"We have all the decorations up looking good," Greta said.

"We need to set the table," Greta said.

"We need enough tables to set up the following:

1st table

Gifts- Place the table near the entrance to the right side of the door entrance.

2nd table

Silverware, napkins, toothpicks, salt, pepper, and pepper sauce- Place those on the table below the kitchen window on the left side of the room, close to the meat table.

3rd table

Meats- Place the table on the left side of the room in the corner.

4th table

Vegetables- Place the table a few feet from the meat table on the back wall.

5th table

Breads- Place the table a few feet from the vegetable table on the back wall.

6th table

Deserts- Place the table on the right side of the room in the corner.

7th table

Drinks- Place the table on the far right side wall close to the dessert table. A punch bowl will be sitting on the table. There will also be some coolers with a variety of cold drinks.

"What time is it?" Diane asked.

"The time is 1:00 p.m.," Greta answered.

"OK, we are still looking good on time," Diane said.

"Diane, will you ask Travis to bring seven tables from the storeroom," Greta asked.

"Sure," Diane said.

"Here you are," Travis said.

"Thanks," Diane said.

"Look in the kitchen on the counter and get the tablecloths and the center-pieces," Greta asked.

"OK," I have them. They are pretty," Diane said.

"I will help you set the tables," Greta said.

"Thanks, there is a lot to decorate," Diane said.

"No problem, you know we work as a team," Greta said.

"You can go to one side of the hall and place the tablecloths and the centerpieces. I will do the same thing on the other side of the aisle. We will meet in the middle, Greta said.

"Good idea," Diane said.

"OK, all the tables are covered," Greta said.

"What is next?" Greta said.

"Do we have balloons?" Diane asked.

"Yes," Greta replied.

"They are in the corner already blown up," Diane said.

"Put a few stringed balloons on the corner of the tables. Please take a few and place them on the walls of the room. Count how many balloons are left, and we will determine where we can place the leftover balloons. Do not forget to put some on the decorated birthday chair," Diane said.

"You think we have enough to do all that?" Diane asked.

"If not, I am sure Travis would not mind blowing up a few more balloons," Greta said.

"How are we on time?" Greta asked.

"The time is 2:00 p.m.," Diane answered.

"The time is getting close," Greta said.

"Yes, it is," Diane said.

"Do we have punch?" Diane asked.

"Yes, I have everything on the cabinet to your right. The punch bowl is in the sink," Travis said.

"Diane washed the punch bowl and dipper. I will get the ingredients together," Greta said.

"OK," Diane said.

The girls mixed the ingredients and added the ice.

Diane asked Travis to taste the punch.

Travis tasted the punch. He said to add more sugar.

We added more sugar.

We asked Travis to taste the punch one more time.

"It tastes just right," Travis said.

The girls asked Travis to pick up the punch bowl and place it on the table next to the dessert.

Travis placed the punch bowl in the right place on the table.

"Thank you," Diane said.

Diane placed several cups of ice on the table. She also put some mints, nuts, and peppermints on the table.

"We need to start placing the food on the tables," Diane said.

"Yes, you are correct," Greta said.

"I am headed towards the kitchen, Diane. You want to follow me so we can work on one table at a time?" Greta asked.

"Yes, on my way," Diane said.

"I will place the pot of chicken on the table. You can pick up the pot with the sausage, and we can assist with the ribs tray. Does that sound good to you?" Greta asked.

"Sure sounds good to me," Diane said.

"Do you want to lead in carrying the ribs to the table?" Greta asked.

"Sure, I will get on the right, and you can get on the left. That way, the weight will possibly be even," Diane said.

"Girls, that looks heavy. Call me when it is too much for you. Do not want you to hurt yourselves. Here, let me carry this. Where do you want it," Travis asked.

Please place it on the table to your left in the corner with the rest of the meats," Greta said.

"Thanks," they both replied.

"OK, the meat table is complete," Diane said.

"Yes, with the help of Travis," Greta said.

"So true," Diane said.

The vegetables should not be that heavy," Greta said.

"I agree the dishes are not that large," Diane said.

We will place the green beans, yams, corn, and red beans on one side of the table. The potato salad and the broccoli casserole will be put together on the other side of the table.

"I hope you know what you are talking about," Diane said.

"I got this. It will work," Greta said.

"Are we good with the veggies?" Diane asked.

"Let us stand back and look at the table. Everything will be OK as long as the trays are not too close to the table's edge," Greta said.

"Yes, it looks good," they both replied.

"Greta, you are so creative you can make things come together. It is amazing. I do not know how you do it," Diane said.

"We are doing this together. Not just me being creative. You are also in this picture. I am not going to take all the credit. We are in this together. Let us continue to make it happen for the guest of honor, family, and friends," Greta said.

"OK, let us keep it moving. We have more food to place on the tables for the party," Diane said.

"Put the bread on the next table," Greta said.

"We have a variety of breads. We should be able to fit them on the table," Diane said.

"Looks good," Diane asked.

"I agree it looks good," Greta said.

"You are so smart," Diane said.

"Thank you, Diane. We are both smart because we are working on this project together," Greta said.

"We need to go to the kitchen and get the desserts," Diane said.

"Set the cakes on one side and the pies on the other," Greta said.

"We can place the cookies in the middle around the cakes and pies," Diane said.

"I am with you," Greta said.

"I think we have everything set," Greta said.

"I think so, too," Diane said.

"Let us stand back and see how everything looks," Diane said.

"OK," Greta said.

"Travis, what do you think?" Greta asked.

"It looks great," Travis answered.

"Now let's go over here so I can show you how to work the music system and the location of the DVDs. My Dad made sure there were various DVDs to choose from. He said you can play whatever you like. He also has a birthday song he wants you to play when we get together for the ceremonial part of the birthday party. You think you can handle it?" Travis asked.

"Yes, I can handle it," Greta answered.

"OK, Greta, you get in your DJ spot, and Diane, you can go behind the meats and veggies table to serve everyone. The people can serve their desserts and drinks," Travis said.

People started coming in 30 minutes early while we were still getting things together.

Before we realized the time was 3:00 p.m.

"I will put some soft music on until the crowd or guest of honor arrives," Greta said.

Diane was standing at her post, ready to serve people.

Around 3:30 p.m., Travis's Mom and father arrived.

Travis helped his Mom to her chair. She asked what was going on.

"Well, Mom, we decided to give you a surprise birthday party," Travis said.

"I thought I was attending a meeting," Mom said.

"You are," Travis said.

"It has been too quiet in my house this week. I am used to listening to the radio in the back of the house. Travis plays his radio down low every day. My husband usually is in the garage working on one of his projects. I knew something was up," Mom said.

"I guess all this week, they have been getting things together for this occasion," Mom said.

"Yes, Mom, we all have been busy getting things ready for the party," Travis said.

"It takes time to plan a party. You have to put your thinking cap on," Travis said.

Travis socialized a little with his Mom and Dad. He left them and started mingling with the other visitors.

At 4:00 p.m., Travis announced that everybody was here today to honor his Mom, Mrs. Hines's birthday. He held his hand over his Mom's head in case people did not know his Mom. However, anybody could tell if you are sitting in a decorated chair, you are the guest of honor.

"Let us sing happy birthday to my Mom," Travis said.

Everyone joined in and sang Happy Birthday to Mrs. Hines. She was smiling. She felt good that everyone came out to celebrate her birthday.

When they finished, Travis told everyone to get in line to be served.

Travis walked with his Mom and father to the table to get something to eat. Travis made sure his Mom received her food first.

Travis's Dad was in line to get his food. Oops, I forgot something in the car. I'll be back. He left the cake in the car.

"Dad," Travis said.

Dad went to the car to get the cake. It was a large cake for one person to carry.

Dad walked in the door with the cake. It looked like he was struggling to carry the cake. Travis hurried to assist his Dad with the cake. Travis and his Dad brought the cake unnoticed to the kitchen and placed it on the counter. Travis and his father knew they needed another table to set the cake close to the dessert table. They quickly set up a table, placed the cake on it, and got back in line.

Everybody looked settled, eating, socializing, and listening to music.

"Who is playing the music, and who is the young lady serving at the table?" Mom asked.

"They are Travis's friends," Dad said.

"They are doing a great job. You make sure to tell them I said so," Mom said.

"I will," Dad said.

"It is time to cut the cake," Travis said.

Mom walked to the table. Diane allowed Travis's Mom to get the knife and cut the first piece of cake. Then, Travis got the knife and gave it to Diane so she could cut some cake for everyone. This would eliminate the cake being cut in all different ways.

Mom walked back to her table with her cake. It was taking a while to get back to her chair. Mom likes to talk to everybody.

Diane stopped cutting the cake because people stopped coming to the table to get a piece. She walked around with a few cake slices in case someone waited until the line went down. Diane was able to get rid of the portion that was in her hand. She stayed behind the table just in case someone needed some. Diane cut a piece of cake for her and Greta.

It was getting close to the end of the party. People started leaving and saying their goodbyes.

Travis's Dad drove his Mom home.

It was time to clean up. We started cleaning up, and Travis was also helping.

We finished cleaning and locked the door. Travis said he would take us home. We got to Diane's house first. She was about to get out when Travis gave Diane an envelope. He said it was from his Dad.

"Thank you," Diane said.

Travis drove to my house. He also gave me an envelope as I exited the car.

"Thank you," Greta said.

"Greta, my family appreciates you and Diane helping us with the birthday party," Travis said.

"You are welcome. Diane and I like doing fun things," Greta said.

"If you do not watch out, you will be doing more of the same thing once the word gets out," Travis said.

"Hum, that is something to think about," Greta said.

"Yes, it is," Travis said.

"See you Monday at school," Greta said.

"Sure will," Travis said.

Greta and Diane could not wait to call each other after they got dropped off at the house.

Since Greta was the last to get dropped off, Diane called Greta several times. No, answer. I guess the phone was on silent during the party.

Greta finally called Diane back.

"I have been calling you," Diane said.

"Sorry my ringer was off," Greta said.

"I figured," Diane said.

"Have you opened your envelope?" Greta asked.

"No," Diane said.

"Have you?" Diane asked.

"No," Greta said.

"Let's open our envelopes together," Diane said.

"OK," Greta said.

50 dollars, Greta said.

50 dollars, Diane said.

"That was nice of Travis and his father," Greta said.

"Yes, it was," Diane said.

On Monday, the girls did their usual routine at school.

The girls got in line to get their lunch. The girls heard some kids whispering about a birthday party this past weekend.

Diane and Greta tried to listen to the conversation, but there was so much noise in the line that they could hardly hear what was being said. They were trying to be so nosy that the lunch lady repeatedly asked them what they wanted to eat, and they did not respond.

Destiny was standing behind Diane and Greta. She told them to turn around. The lunch lady was talking to both of them.

"Stop being nosy. You are holding up the line," Destiny said.

Diane and Greta turned around and made a selection. They paid for their lunch and walked to their table. They noticed their table was full, so they found another table.

They sat down and began to eat their lunch. A few minutes later, a group of kids came over from their original table to our table. Travis was with the group of people that were seated at our table. He was in the front and headed toward us.

"Travis said he enjoyed the party and was glad both of them could take the assignment to help with the party.

"By the way, my Mom asked me to give both of you a message," Travis said.

Diane and Greta looked at one, thinking about what his Mom had to say to us.

"My Mom said both of you did a great job," Travis said.

Diane and Greta gave each other a high five.

The girls with Travis said they wanted Diane and Greta to participate in their party celebrations.

Diane and Greta smiled.

The group walked back to the other table and continued with their conversations.

Diane and Greta thought of having peace with a few minutes left to finish lunch.

The girls quickly ate their lunch and went to class.

When they got home, both parents asked them what they had done at the party this past weekend. The phone has been ringing, and people have been asking questions about when you will be available for future party events. I told them I could not answer that question. You would have to ask the girls. I called Diane's Mom and asked if she got many phone calls about the birthday party?

"Yes," Diane's Mother replied.

Diane and Greta looked at one another and said we needed to determine what we would do with this new project. People already need us to assist them with their events.

Diane and Greta decided they would look into what needs to be done as a business.

The parents did not question the girl's intent to have a business. They just needed to ensure everyone respected both parents' phones and limit stopping by the house.

The girls got everything straight to be able to pursue this career. The girls knew that taking on a business was time-consuming, and they knew that their business could not interfere with school obligations.

The girls continued to do parties during school, summer, and graduation. They were unsure if they wanted to continue after graduation with the possibility of attending college out of town.

THE FOX AND
THE HOUND

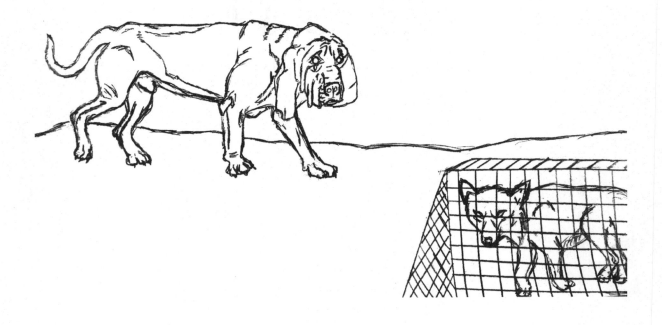

THE STORY IS ABOUT TWO animals that came to be best friends.

The Fox name is Jasper, and the Hounds name is Duffus.

The story begins in a small town where pretty flowers, ground scenery, hills, and mountains are as tall as the eyes can see.

There are a lot of farmlands animals, such as sheep, goats, ducks and chickens, and turkeys.

There is no limit to what you might see in this small town of Fritzberg.

The town has been in existence for a pretty long time. It is known to have yearly festivals to bring the community together before winter comes in.

The town has a store that makes candles. They are open all year round. They have a locomotive train that goes around on the track in the ceiling. You can see it move around and make the train noise as you shop in the store.

The town holds a two-day dance so the people can let their hair down and enjoy themselves with people they know and those new to the city.

The town holds various events such as pie, chili, and barbeque contests.

The town has fox hunts and horse racing events.

A few townsmen decided to do a trial run on a fox hunt one day.

Mr. Bannon is the counsel administrator for the town.

A group of men went to an open range outside of town to see if the dogs could hunt and fetch a fox.

Mr. Bannon will be present to make sure everything runs smoothly.

Everyone should have at least one to two dogs for the event.

Mr. Bannon brought four dogs. He has two of his dogs in training.

Winners will receive various prizes for their participation. Even though the trial run is a practice run, hunters take the event seriously.

Mr. Bannon got everyone together and provided the instructions that would take place in the event.

"Come on, Mr. Bannon, we know the rules," The hunters said.

"I have to practice my speech for the real event," Mr. Bannon said.

"Ok," said the hunters.

The hunters were anxious to begin the race. They were getting chesty.

I wonder what the fox was thinking. Was he thinking, take your time? Or did the fox have something up his sleeve?

The fox's name is Jasper. Jasper is pretty smart to be a fox.

Jasper plans on getting out of the fox hunt business.

The time has come, Mr. Bannon, to allow the fox to be released. The hunters let their dogs loose. The dogs are running all different ways to locate the Fox. After giving the Fox a few minutes', Mr. Bannon pulled the trigger on the gun.

Jasper was waiting a little while to see the dogs' directions. He was still figuring out how he was going to get away.

Jasper decided what he was going to do. He would make the dogs think he got scared and did not want to run because he was tired.

Jasper ran a little more. He knew the dogs were getting tired.

Jasper saw a log. He figured that would be an excellent spot to get caught.

He hid in the bark of the old log until the dogs finally came.

The dogs finally picked up his scent. They saw him in the log looking at them. Jasper said to himself, "You dummies come and get me."

Jasper purposely hid in that log because it would not be far from his next run and trick he would play on the dogs.

Mr. Bannon announced that the dogs had found the fox.

Mr. Bannon brought the cage for the fox. He picked up Jasper and placed him in it. Mr. Bannon made sure the fox was safe for the final run.

The event allowed an hour's break before the actual hunt event.

This break allowed Jasper to figure out how he would get away.

Jasper noticed that all the dogs came at one time instead of one or two than the rest.

Jasper also noticed the hunters were far away before the dogs could pick up his scent.

Jasper had plans to run closer to the road and cut through the creek for the next run. He knew the dogs would lose his scent and continue to look to see if someone would be driving on the road.

Jasper wanted a big gap between the dogs for enough time to escape.

It was time for the main event.

Jasper was ready to get this over. He's running for freedom and can hardly wait not to be a part of a fox hunting event. He knew after this event, Mr. Bannon would have to get another fox for next year's event.

"Yea," Jasper thought.

Mr. Bannon got the hunters together. He opened the cage and let Jasper out.

In a few minutes, Mr. Bannon pulled the trigger on the gun and, off the dogs, went after Jasper.

Jasper ran close to the area where he had planned. He picked up his speed in case he had to make a change.

Jasper continued to have a big gap between him and the dogs. Jasper walked across the creek up and down so the dogs would lose his sent. He walked further up to see if a vehicle was coming up the road. Back in the creek again, trying to confuse the dogs and give him more time to escape. While trying to make sure the dogs were so confused, he heard a noise like an engine on the road. He got out of the creek and noticed an object down the road. Jasper decided he better get closer to the road. Jasper could hear the dogs. He got out of the creek to check it out. There was a vehicle about half a mile away.

Jasper played like he was hurt by lying in the middle of the road. The driver saw Jasper and stopped to see what he could do. The driver approached Jasper. Jasper kicked his leg to let the driver know he was still alive. It so happens that the driver is a Veterinarian.

The man picked Jasper up and placed him in a cage in the back of the truck.

Jasper could hear the dogs getting closer as the vehicle drove away. Jasper wondered if the driver listened to the dogs or was familiar with the tradition in that part of the country.

Jasper's heart was beating fast, "Let's go, let's go. Jasper took a deep breath. He knew he was finally safe.

Jasper was on his way to a different atmosphere. He is looking forward to anything better than where he was. For years Jasper was hunted, and there were some close calls to catching him. Those dogs were mean, and they wanted to take him apart.

"I would love to be a part of a family that treats me nice. I would not be a bother," Jasper said.

The man drove for a little while. He must be from a nearby town.

The truck stopped. The man picked me up in the cage and carried me into a building. He was the only one in the building. His phone was ringing. His wife called and asked where he was? He said he picked up an injured animal on the road, placed it in a cage in the back of his truck and brought the animal to the office. His wife asked whether the animal was still alive? Not sure I just got in the office. I need to examine it first. I will check and see. I will see you when I get home.

"OK," she said.

The man opened the cage and lifted Jasper out. He placed him on the table. The man examined Jasper and noticed his only injury was his leg. Jasper moved his leg like it was hurting. The man lightly wrapped the leg.

Jasper assumed the man thought he hurt his leg. Jasper thought the man did not know that Jasper could pretend when he wanted to.

The man cleaned his work area in the office after tending to Jasper.

The man picked Jasper up and placed him in the cage back in the truck.

The wife called again, asking questions about the animal he found. The man said he was on his way home. He said he was bringing the animal home to monitor his condition.

"OK," said the wife.

The man arrived at his place of residence. He picked Jasper and the cage up. Jasper noticed the house was huge and had a lot of land. The house had a fence around its property. It looked like the animals were in the back of the house.

The man was about to enter the house. In front of the house, Jasper noticed a swing and firewood on the porch.

His wife met us at the door. She was looking at me in the cage. "Is this the animal?" She asked.

"Yes," he answered.

He said it looked like the animal injured his leg, and he should be up and walking in a few days.

"Good," she said.

We walked into the house there was a droopy dog with floppy ears and brown eyes.

He looked at me. Who do you think you are coming to my house.

"I hope we do not cross paths," Jasper was thinking.

The man put me in the washroom on the floor. He closed the door.

Everyone went into the living room. I could hear the man and lady talking.

So far, so good I wonder what their plans are for me. Do I have to play hurt a while to get attention? I hope not.

It seems to be a friendly family.

Where the man placed me was nice and cozy.

The following day the wife gave me food and water.

The man did not come in and check on me. He went to work and told the wife to tend to me. That's ok, Jasper thought.

After I finished eating the wife accidentally left the door open.

I happen to fill something breathing close to my cage. I looked up, and that big Dog was staring at me. I guess he thought he would scare me. I do not scare that easy.

I opened my eyes and asked him whether I could help him. Jasper said.

"I'm looking at you, and what of it?" The Dog said.

"Why are you here?" The Dog asked.

"Duh," as you can see, I'm hurt, Jasper said.

"I bet you are not hurt. You do not look injured," The Dog said.

"Looks can be deceiving. Can't you see I'm hurt?" "Duh," Jasper said.

"You're a smarty pants, aren't you?" The Dog said.

"You can call me whatever you like, but we need to get along in this camp," Jasper answered.

"What is your name?" My name is Jasper.

"What is your name?" My name is Duffus.

"Duffus," Jasper said.

"Are you trying to be funny?" Duffus said.

"NO, If the shoe fits, wear it," Jasper said.

"I'm not sure I understand what you just said," Duffus said.

"That's "OK" you will get over it," Jasper said.

"Hey, how long do you plan on staying here?" Duffus asked.

"At this point, I'm unsure why you ask?" Jasper answered.

"I need to know it is not enough room for two furry animals in this camp," Duffus answered.

"Who made you Marshall of this house?" Jasper said.

"I'm the four-legged authority in this house. I will woof you away if you do not follow my lead," Duffus answered.

"Ooh, I'm scared," Jasper said.

"You talk a lot of smack to someone who cannot do anything right now because of an injury," Jasper said.

"I want to let you know you are second in command, and I am first? "Get it?" Duffus said.

"I get it for right now. You don't know who you are talking to," Jasper said.

Jasper shut up, going back and forth with Duffus until he could break the ice and show Duffus to back off.

Jasper let Duffus have his say.

Jasper did not say anything else. He turned his back to Duffus and played as if he was asleep.

Duffus walked out the door, saying now that is how you are supposed to act.

Jasper turned around with one eye open, thinking you did not know you got it coming.

Several hours past Jasper did not hear anything in the house. He was wondering where everyone was. He eventually listened to a small voice. A boy came into the room. His Mom called him Jimmy. Jimmy stared at Jasper and asked if his Mom would allow him to play. His Mom asked him to wait a few days because the animal was injured.

"OK," Jimmy said.

Several days passed, and the Mom continued to feed and give Jasper water.

The Mom said it was time for Jasper to remove the bandage and walk around the house.

Jimmy came home from school and asked if it was OK to play with the animal.

The Mom said, yes, it is "OK" to play with the animal. Just be careful how you handle him.

Jimmy picked Jasper up and went outside in the backyard. Jimmy laid Jasper on the ground.

Jasper pretended to walk like he was just taking his first steps. Jasper walked around and laid down. He was feeling good about himself.

Jimmy allowed Jasper to stay outside for about thirty minutes.

Jimmy's Mom called Jimmy to bring the animal back into the house.

Duffus was peeping around the corner the whole time. Duffus walked upon Jasper. By that time, before anything could happen between the two. Jimmy came back outside to take the animal back inside.

Jimmy told Duffus he better be nice to the animal.

Duffus had his head down as he walked toward the barn. He quickly turned around, passed the tractor, and bent down, peeping at Jimmy and Jasper.

The man came home from work. He came outside through the kitchen to see how the animal was adjusting.

He asked Jimmy how things were going.

"OK," Jimmy said.

The bandage will be taken off tomorrow and at that time. I will decide what to do with the animal.

Jimmy asked his parents if he could keep the animal.

The man did not respond. He said we would see tomorrow.

"OK," Jimmy said.

Duffus determined two could play at this game.

The next day Jimmy let Jasper out and went back into the house. Jimmy left Jasper out a little longer than usual. You think that Jimmy was testing the relationship between Jasper and Duffus.

Duffus saw Jasper lying in his spot. Duffus was about to walk toward Jasper. He decided to step in between two barrels with crates on top of them. The barrels fell on Duffus's leg. Duffus barked loud with pain. Jasper got up to see what happened. Duffus told him what happened. Jasper ran and scratched the back door. He howled as loud as he could. The man just came home from work. He heard a noise in the backyard. He ran to see what was going on. Jasper showed the man where Duffus laid hurt. The man took Duffus to his office to help Duffus with his injury.

The next time I saw Duffus, he had something white on his leg.

The man put Duffus in a cage to keep him from hurting himself.

I went to peep at Duffus. "What goes up must come down," "Now you see how I felt," Jasper said.

"Yes, I see how it feels," Duffus said.

"Truce," Duffus said.

"Truce," Jasper said.

"Since you will be out of commission for a while, let's get acquainted," Jasper said.

"Sounds good to me," Duffus said.

"Does this mean we will be friends?"Duffus asked.

"Yes," this means we will be friends," Jasper answered.

"That's good. It is nice to have friends," Duffus said.

"If you only knew," Jasper said to himself.

It was confirmed that Jimmy could keep the animal. Jimmy' was told to keep up with his chores and grades at school. "You now have two animals to tend to might not be as easy as you think. But if you need some help, he would be more than happy to assist," Jimmy's Dad said.

"Thanks," Jimmy said.

"Well, Duffus, it is approved. I will be part of the family. Is that Ok with you?" Jasper asked.

"Yes," Duffus replied.

"Thanks for allowing me to be a part of your family," Jasper said.

"You are welcome," Duffus said.

There is nothing like having friends. A friend in need is a friend indeed."

TRACY FINDS A FRIEND

Tracey is eight years old, and she is in the third grade. She attends Winery Elementary School in Dallas, Texas.

Have you ever thought about having a friend who will be a person you could trust and even confined with your deep thoughts and secrets?

Everyone needs someone they can talk to other than their parents or family. You can share things, prepare for the unknown, and grow up together.

People in general and their family members put down stakes for a few years, then they move. This makes the children leave their friends with the thought of never seeing them again.

This story begins with a young girl named Tracey. She is a quiet young lady who longs to have a friend to play with, like a sister.

Tracey has friends to play with at school and in the neighborhood. She stays to herself.

She socializes in school activities but still thinks having a true sister would be awesome. She has a brother named Nathan, who is too young to understand. He's five months old. Googoo and Gigi's baby talk is not what I call a conversation.

It will take a long time before he can talk to me. I make sounds to make him laugh, but does he really understand? That is a good question.

My brother has time to grow up, have fun, and learn about people for himself.

I'm much older than he is, but I still have much to learn.

I wish I had a sister. I dare not ask my mother to have a sister for me because I cannot play with her like I want to. I will be in the same boat with my little baby brother.

I better get ready for bed. I have school tomorrow.

Tracey did what she needed to do to get ready for bed.

Tracey heard her mother walk past her door. She told her good night.

Tracey fell asleep quickly. She did not realize how tired she was.

The next thing Tracey felt was a slight shove on her shoulder, saying, Wake up. It's time to get ready for school. When Tracey heard those words, she knew it was not a dream, and she better wake up.

Tracey woke up and realized it was her Mom waking her with the alarm clock. Tracey's Mom said wake up. Your alarm is going off.

Tracey jumped up, thinking she was late for school. She looked at the clock. She had plenty of time to get ready for school.

You must have been in a deep sleep. Did you not hear me or the alarm clock? Mom asked.

Yes, I was tired, but thank you, Mom, for waking me up. I might have been late for school, and I don't like being late for anything.

"Yes, I know," Mom said.

"Mom, have you seen my yellow socks? I can't find them?" Tracey asked.

"I thought I saw them in the washroom," Mom said.

"In the washroom, Mom, are you sure they are clean?" Tracey asked.

"As far as I know, they're washed and dried," Mom said.

OK, Tracey said.

"I'll look for them while you finish getting dressed," Mom said.

"Are you almost ready for school?" Mom asked.

"I'm ready," Tracey said.

"Hurry, I see the bus driving up to the bus stop," Mom said.

"I'm heading out the door right now," Tracey said.

"OK, have a good day," Mom said.

"I will," Tracey said.

She walked onto the bus, and the bus door was shut. The Driver continued driving the children to their school.

Mrs. Fletcher greeted all the students at the door before entering the classroom. I put my stuff in my locker and went to the board to move my name to show I was present. I looked around to see if my classmates to my right and left had made it to school. Amber and David had not made it to school by the time I left the board. I noticed David and Amber heading toward their locker to put their stuff up.

Susan's chair was close to the board. She walked over to my desk and said good morning.

"Good morning," I replied.

I assumed everyone was accounted for. The teacher shut the door and said good morning to the class. Good morning, Mrs. Fletcher, we all replied.

The class listened to the announcements and started their morning warm-up work.

There was a knock on the door. Mr. Lucky, the Assistant Principal, was at the door with a student and a parent.

Mrs. Fletcher asked them to come in. Mrs. Fletcher asked the class if they knew who was in the classroom this morning.

Yes, Mr. Lucky, the Assistant Principal.

How do you give respect to Mr. Lucky? Mrs. Fletcher asked.

The whole class said good morning, Mr. Lucky,

"Good morning," Mr. Lucky said.

"Mr. Lucky came to introduce a new student to the classroom and school. What is the school song for new students?" Mr. Lucky asked.

All the students stood up and sang the welcome school song.

"It is a pleasure for you to be a part of Winery Elementary. We are looking forward to making you as comfortable as possible. Welcome from Winery Elementary," Mr. Lucky said.

The students sat down after they sang the welcome song.

Mrs. Fletcher and Mr. Lucky applauded for such an excellent job in singing the Welcome School song.

Mr. Lucky introduced the student (Casey) and parent, Mrs. Day, to the class.

Mrs. Fletcher shook Casey's and Mrs. Day's hands, welcoming them to the classroom and school.

Mrs. Fletcher let Casey know she'll be her teacher.

Mr. Lucky stayed briefly, and then Mrs. Day kissed Casey. She said she'll see her after school at the location they discussed this morning.

Mr. Lucky and Mrs. Day left the classroom, walking toward the office.

Mrs. Fletcher walked to the cabinet and removed a beautiful sack from the bottom. She gave it to Casey.

"Thank you," Casey said.

Mrs. Fletcher showed Casey where she would be sitting. There was an empty desk close to Mrs. Fletcher's desk.

Mrs. Fletcher asked the helper to get Casey a new daily supply bucket. It so happened that Tracey was the helper for the day.

Tracey pulled the supply bucket, material package, and book for Casey. She walked the items to Casey.

"Thank you," Casey said.

"You're welcome," Tracey said.

Mrs. Fletcher made a name tag for Casey. It was placed on her locker, desk, and board. Mrs. Fletcher asked Tracey to come to her desk and pick up the items for Casey.

Tracey showed Casey where to place the name tags.

Mrs. Fletcher continued with the morning assignment.

Since Casey is new to this school, the helper should help her for a few days to get familiar with the school grounds.

Tracey says Casey seems to adjust pretty well to her new school surroundings. I think she got it.

The following Monday, the students entered the classroom and noticed the teacher had cupcakes on her desk. It has been a long time since we had cupcakes for class appreciation.

Everyone was settled in class, and the door was closed.

"Mrs. Fletcher made an announcement she had a surprise. Casey's mother made the class some cupcakes. She wanted to thank you for such a warm welcome from Casey to the students in her homeroom. She also brought some small drinks. What are we going to say, class?" Mrs. Fletcher asked.

"Thank you, Casey," the class responded.

The class lined up by the door to use the sanitizer before eating. Then, the students returned to their desks.

Mrs. Fletcher passed out the cupcakes. Casey passed out the drinks.

While everyone was eating, Mrs. Fletcher selected a book given to her by another parent.

Mrs. Fletcher selected a story from the book. She paused and asked the students questions. The students responded by raising their hands.

I started reading the story. I stopped often and asked a few questions to ensure they were alert. I told them if I could not finish the story. I would continue at another time.

Everyone was so quiet they actually were interested in the story. I continued to read, and then I had to stop to return to the lesson plan.

Casey asked Mrs. Fletcher the Author's name. Mrs. Fletcher wrote the Author's name and gave it to Casey.

"Thank you," Casey said.

"I hope you and your family will enjoy the book," Mrs. Fletcher said.

"I'm sure we will," Casey said.

Mrs. Fletcher reminded everyone to clean their area so they could start on the following action for class.

Casey was smiling all day.

"Are you OK?" Tracey asked.

"Yes, the story was so interesting. I really enjoyed it," Casey said.

"OK, I thought it was something else," Tracey said.

"No, I liked the story. That was all," Casey said.

"OK," Tracey said.

As the day went on, Mrs. Fletcher finished the actions that needed to be taken care of on her daily planner.

The students started getting ready to go home. Several students went to Mrs. Fletcher to tell her they enjoyed the story.

Mrs. Fletcher said since she received so many compliments about the story. She would finish the story and let the class pick another one from the book.

"Yeah," Casey said.

Mrs. Fletcher looked at Casey and said that Casey was finally opening up.

The students left the classroom, saying goodbye to the teacher and classmates. They said they'll see each other tomorrow.

Tracey got home from school, did her homework, and cleaned the house. She had something fun on her mind but wasn't sure how she would get permission from her mother to allow the activity.

Tracey's mother was in the kitchen.

Tracey started doing things to impress her mother before she popped the question.

Tracey went to the kitchen and got a glass of water. She sat at the table and decided it was to do or die.

"Something is up, Mom said. Usually, you will still be doing something in your room. What do you have up your sleeve?"

"Mom, I have had something on my mind to ask you, but I did not know how to ask you," Tracey said.

"Tracey, you will never know until you ask. Either I will say YES, NO, or let me think about it," Mom said.

"OK, Mom. You know I do not have many friends, just kids at school. I thought having a slumber party would be a good idea," Tracey said.

"Was that hard to ask?" Mom asked.

"Yes, I was really nervous," Tracey said.

"Tracey, that is a good idea," Mom said.

"When would you like to have a sleepover?" Mom asked.

"This Saturday, That only gives you a few days to prepare," Mom said.

Let's get things started. We need a list of items from the store.

"It's not too late to make a list tonight and go to the store tonight," Mom said.

"Let's make a list now. Go in the hall closet and get me a tablet," Mom said.

"You want some hot chocolate while we get things together?" Mom asked.

"Yes," Tracey said.

"We need pizza, hot dogs, buns, mustard, ketchup, relish, chips, drinks, and cookies. Are you going to play games?" Mom asked.

"What do you think?" Tracey asked.

"It is left up to you. It is your party," Mom said.

"We have plenty of games in the loft," Mom said.

"OK," Tracey said.

"What about gift bags and invitation cards," Mom said.

"OK," Tracey said.

"Well, Tracey, since we have the list ready, why not make a trip to Walmart," Mom said.

"Now, Mom," Tracey said.

"Yes, Now," Mom said.

"It is best to get what you can to see if you missed anything before the event," Mom said.

"Let me get my purse," Mom said.

"OK, I'm ready," Mom said.

"Wal-Mart has a party area. We can go straight to that area and get what we need," Mom said.

They arrive at Wal-Mart.

"I will go get the snacks, and you get what you need from the party area in the store," Mom said.

"OK," Tracey said.

"OK, Tracey, I think I have everything we need for the party," Mom said.

"How far have you gotten on the things you need for the party?" Mom asked.

"Let me check what you have if you do not mind?" Mom asked.

"Looks good. Put everything in this big basket," Mom said.

"OK, we are heading to the checkout stand," Mom said.

"OK," Tracey said.

"When we get to the house, bring everything to the kitchen table so we can line everything out and make out your invitations," Mom said.

"When do you want to have the party, and how many of your friends will be attending the party?" Mom asked.

"I want to have it Saturday, and only five girls will attend the party," Tracey said.

"Do you think this is short notice?" Mom asked.

"No, I pretty well know the girls, and they do not have anything pending that would keep them from attending the party," Tracey said.

"Thanks, Mom, for your encouragement," Tracey said.

"You're welcome. I'm just trying to keep you encouraged that the party will turn out just fine," Mom said.

"Let's go through the list," Mom said.

"We will have pizza from Little Caesars. The dessert comes with the family order. We brought sodas and some extra drinks from the pantry. We have chips, cookies, and candy. We have gift bags. We have the games in the loft. The only thing left is the invitations," Mom said.

"I have a music box, and we can watch movies on Netflix," Tracey said.

"Do you need help preparing the invitation list?" Mom asked.

"No, I'm good," Tracey said.

"What time should I put on the invitation? and what time is pickup?" Tracey asked.

"You should allow the girls enough time to do their chores before they come over," Mom said.

"So the party will be Friday from 7:00 p.m. to Saturday until 12:00 noon," Tracey said.

"You changed the day and time?" Mom asked.

"I felt like the girls might want to attend church on Sunday. So I did not want to interfere with family plans," Tracey said.

"That was considerate," Mom said.

"Well, Mom, we have everything we need for the party. We reviewed the food list, gift bags, games, and invitation cards. Can you think of anything else?" Tracey asked.

"No, sounds like you got everything under control. You have to remember to put the invitation cards in a good place. You do not want to forget them," Mom said.

"I will not forget them," Tracey

said.

"Do you have the gift bags ready?" Mom asked.

"No, I will prepare them before I go to bed," Tracey said.

"Are all the girls in your homeroom or another classroom?" Mom asked.

"No, everybody is in my homeroom. I will give everyone invitations tomorrow," Tracey said.

"Mom, you want to see my list of all the girls attending the party?" Tracey asked.

"Sure, let me check to ensure you spelled the names correctly," Mom said.

"Mom, I know how to spell," Tracey said.

"I'm not saying you do not know how to spell, but errors happen," Mom said.

"OK, here is the list and envelopes," Tracey said.

"OK, everything looks good. I have a question. I noticed a name on one of the girls you have on the list. Who is Casey?" Mom asked.

"Why do you ask?" Tracey asked.

"Just curious," Mom said.

"She is a new student enrolled in our school several months ago," Tracey said.

"What is her mother's name?" Mom asked.

"Her mother's name is Mrs. Day," Tracey said.

"Mrs. Day, you said?" Mom asked.

"Yes, Mrs. Day and her daughter's name is Casey," Tracey said.

"Why, Mom, do you know them?" Tracey asked.

"The name sounds familiar," Mom said.

"Well, I will be available in case you need me tomorrow. I will go to the loft and get the games. I will put them in the hall closet so you can pull them out when needed," Mom said.

"Do you have the same gifts in all the gift bags?" Mom asked.

"No, I have different things in the gift bags," Tracey said.

"Which bag is for Casey?" Mom asked.

"It is the yellow bag. I like yellow, so I picked yellow for Casey," Tracey said.

"I want to put something extra in Casey's bag. Do not ask me why," Mom said.

"OK," Tracey said.

"Mom, you do not know Casey? Why are you putting an extra gift in her bag? What is the real deal?" Tracey asked.

"Young lady, what did I tell you not to do?" Mom said.

"Zilch my bag. Sorry, Mom," Tracey said.

"OK, Tracey, it is time for you to get ready for bed," Mom said.

"OK, Mom, on my way. Mom, do we have relatives I can play with close by?" Tracey asked.

"No, not that I know of. But you never know. It could change overnight," Mom said.

"Maybe after the slumber party, you will have someone from the group who might spend more time with you instead of just school. I do not mind having a few of your friends spend the night sometimes," Mom said.

"Thanks, Mom. I think having the slumber party will let me know about my friends. I will see how they act away from school and home," Tracey said.

"I agree," Mom said.

"So go in your room and fill the gift bags before it gets too late. It would help if you were not tired and sleepy in the morning. So good night," Mom said.

"Good night," Tracey said.

Everyone went to bed.

Tracey got up before her mother the following day and fixed breakfast. She made oatmeal toast and juice.

Tracey's mother got up and was so surprised. Tracey got up early after trying to put things together for the party. She looked wide awake and ready to go to school.

We both sat at the table, said grace, and ate breakfast.

"Are you ready?" Mom asked.

"I think so," Tracey said.

"Well, now or never, the party is getting closer, so just be calm and breathe," Mom said.

"OK, Mom," Tracey said.

"Finish your breakfast and go to school. I'm sure everything will be fine. I'm here for you. Don't worry. Everything will work out so that this will be the best party you ever had," Mom said.

Tracey finished breakfast, cleaned her area, went to her room, and tidied up. She checked her backpack for the invitations. They're in the side pocket.

Tracey gave her Mom a kiss and a hug as she was leaving out the door to school.

Mom said wait a minute, let's pray together this morning.

"I want you to believe the best is yet to come. You will overcome all obstacles. Now, God will answer our prayers as we hold hands and pray from the heart.

Lord God, as Tracey and I go on our daily routine, help us make good decisions and fight our battle in the storm. Please help us to treat our friends and family right. In Jesus' name, we pray, Amen. You and I have prayed the prayer of faith. We believe everything will be alright. So you go to school in good spirit, and the Lord will comfort and guide you," Mom said.

"Thanks, Mom. I'm ready to tackle my day," Tracey said.

Tracey went out the door to school. She looked like she was ready to tackle the day with encouragement. She had a smile on her face like I got this.

Mom said goodbye and have a good day.

Tracey walked out the door. She was almost at school and saw Naomi walking on the opposite side of the street. She came across the street so she could walk with Tracey to school. Naomi is Tracey's classmate. Tracey gave Naomi her invitation to the party. Naomi said thank you and that she will be there.

Both girls walked into the school building door together and continued to the classroom. Mrs. Fletcher is always standing at the door. She said good morning to both of them as they entered the classroom. Both replied Good Morning.

They both put their backpacks up and sat down at their desk. The morning announcements had not started. Mrs. Fletcher was still standing at the door.

Tracey decided to pass out the rest of the invitations. She asked the teacher if she could pass out some invitations to her slumber party.

Mrs. Fletcher said it was OK.

Tracey started passing out the rest of the invitations. She said she hoped that they could attend. She returned to her desk and had a seat.

Tracey felt good about passing out her inventions. She had a good spirit all day. She concentrated on her work and did what she usually does daily in school.

During lunch, gym, and recess, the girls attending the party were in their little hurdles the whole day talking about girl things like what they would wear and do at the party.

After lunch, everybody went back to class.

Everyone had received their invitation and made plans to attend the Friday outing.

The school was almost out. The girls given invitations were walking out of the class to go home.

Tracey told the girls that she looked forward to seeing them Friday.

The girls walked out of the school building in different directions to go home.

Tracey walked home by herself. The girls must have gotten a ride or walked home fast to share the news about the slumber party with their parents.

Either way, I was almost home.

"As I got to the sidewalk, Mom opened the front door. How was your day?" Mom asked.

"Everything went perfectly," Tracey said.

"Are you ready?" Mom asked.

"Yes. I'm ready. Mom can't wait to get things started," Tracey said.

"OK. Let's go over the list when you get settled. Do you have any homework?" Mom asked.

"No, the teacher did not give us any homework today," Tracey said.

"Where is the list?" Mom asked.

"I have it. It's in my bedroom on my dresser," Tracey said.

"OK, I'm going to relax in the living room. When you get ready, just come in, and we will make final plans," Mom said.

Tracey came into the living room with the list. They both reviewed it. Nothing else needed to be done.

"I'll clean up a little before you know the girls will be here. I need to pull things from the loft," Mom said.

"I think I will cook some spaghetti to go with the pizza," Mom said.

"Good idea," Tracey said.

"Can you think of anything else you might need?" Mom asked.

"No, Mom, you go get the things out from the loft and cook the spaghetti before it gets late, and by that time, the girls will be here," Tracey said.

"OK, on my way to the loft should not take me long. I have everything in a bag?" Mom said.

"Tracey, what time did you tell the girls to come to the party?" Mom asked.

"7:00 p.m.," Tracey said.

"OK, here is the bag with the games in it. I'll put the bag in the living room closet so you can pull it out when you get ready," Mom said.

"On my way to the kitchen to make the spaghetti. My meat is already thawed out. I need to season and cook it a little. Then, put it and the spaghetti in the pot. I will make some garlic bread to accompany it," Mom said.

"Mom, we have about two hours before it will be 7:00, so take your time," Tracey said.

"I have everything ready for the party. The food is ready, drinks are in the cooler, and games are in the closet. All we need is the pizza," Mom said.

"OK, what have you gotten done?" Mom asked.

I made a list of games we can play:

1. Name the Teacher.

2. Headache or Trouble.

3. Feeley Meeley.

4. Mystery date.

5. Monopoly.

6. Hungry Hungry Hippos.

7. Chutes and ladders.

8. Operation.

"I'm sure we will not be able to play all of them, but at least we can pick and choose," Tracey said.

"We will play two games of each. Then we will look at a movie. Do you have any popcorn?" Tracey asked.

"Yes," Mom said.

"OK, we will have popcorn during the movie. Is it OK to eat the popcorn in the living room?" Tracey asked.

"Well, as long as the girls are not too messy, you will have to clean up behind them," Mom said.

"OK," Mom said.

"What about cards games Old-Maid and Go Fish?" Mom asked.

"I planned on playing those games in my room," Tracey said.

"OK," Mom said.

"I have the gift bags in your room in the closet. I chose your room for privacy in case the girls start moving around and happen to see them before I pass them out," Tracey said.

"Where is everybody going to sleep?" Mom asked.

I will tell Casey I would like us to sleep in separate bunk beds in my room. I have an extra roll-a-way bed and two sleeping bags.

"Yes, it is pretty simple. We have a big room with plenty of space. We might even play some other board games. We will see how it flows," Tracey said.

"Mom, can you make me a bowl of candy and put it in my room on the dresser?" Tracey asked.

"Yes, I will do it right now," Mom said.

"OK, Done," Mom said.

"OK, Is anything else that needs to be done on your list?" Mom asked.

"Tracey, I think it is time for both of us to sit and relax until the guest comes," Mom said.

"OK, let us wait in the living room. We have 30 minutes left," Mom said.

"Tracey, I would like to know more about Casey. Where did she previously live?" Mom asked.

"Mom, what is going on about Casey? You sure do have interest in her," Tracey said.

"I have reasons I will share with you before the night ends," Mom said.

Tracey was curious why her Mom kept asking about the new student, Casey. She said she would tell her why she was curious about Casey tonight. She has only been in our school for a few months. My Mom likes her and has never met her as far as I know. What is really up? Hum, time will tell.

"Tracey, someone is at the door," Mom said.

"HI, it is Casey. Her Dad dropped her off," Tracey said.

"Mom, this is Casey," Tracey said.

Hi, I'm Tracey's mother.

"Pleased to me to meet you," Casey said.

"You are pretty like my mother," Casey said.

"Thank you," Tracey's Mom said.

Tracey told Casey to have a seat in the living room.

Casey was staring at Tracey's Mom like she had seen her somewhere.

Tracey's Mom could see she was staring, but Casey was not aware she was staring pretty hard at Tracey's mother.

Tracey's Mom walked into the living room while Tracey was looking out the window for the rest of the girls. She was still staring, and Tracey's Mom wanted Casey to be comfortable.

"Are you OK?" Tracey's Mom asked.

"I'm just puzzled about what you and my mother look like. Are we related?" Casey asked.

"I'm not sure," Tracey's Mom said.

"Both of you could pass for sisters," Casey said.

"My family just recently moved to this town. As we know, we have no relatives here," Casey said. "We are trying to settle in. I'm trying to adjust to the new school and my surroundings. I do not hang out with anybody else since I'm new to the school and the town," Casey said.

"I know how you feel. You will adjust. Just make yourself comfortable. My family used to travel often, so my twin sister and I always made friends wherever we moved. You are with family," Tracey's Mom said.

Family, what? Tracey's Mom has something up her sleeve. Does she have vibes that Casey could be related to?

Casey looked like she was about to ask Tracey's Mom a question, then the doorbell rang. The rest of the girls finally showed up.

Tracey introduced the other girls to her mother. She said Hello, come in and sit in the living room. We will be right with you.

We heard another knock at the door.

"Everybody is here. Who could be at the door?" Tracey asked.

Tracey opened the door. It was Mrs. Williams, our neighbor from next door.

"HI," Mrs. Williams said.

"HI, Mrs. Williams," Tracey said.

"I brought the girls some cupcakes and cookies. I heard you were having a slumber party, and I remembered those days when I had slumber parties for my girls. So I made a few sweets for the occasion," Mrs. Williams said.

Tracey and one of the girls put the treats on the kitchen table.

Tracey and Tracey's Mom said thank you and hugged Mrs. Williams.

"Bye and enjoy," Mrs. Williams said.

Tracey closed the door.

"Mom, that was so nice of her to do that for us, Tracey said.

"Tracey never thought people would show kindness when you just speak in passing. She is our neighbor, but she has a good heart, and she blessed us out of the kindness of her heart," Mom said.

"OK, Mom, that was sweet of her. I will return the kindness and start checking on her," Tracey said.

Tracey went into the living room and told the girls she was glad they could make it to the slumber party. She said she had a list of things they could do, and if they chose, they could change it.

Everybody went to the kitchen, and Mom pulled the games from the closet. She put the games near the window out the way. Tracey went to the bag and pulled out two games, headache and trouble.

Tracey reviewed her list of things to do and the rules for the Teacher name game. It would help if you raised your hand. Do not Yell out the answer.

Tracey explained the rules and asked whether there were any questions. No one answered.

What teacher says the following?

1. Get in line. If I tell you more than once, you will be asked to go to the end of the line.

    (Mrs. Anderson)

2. Tuck your shirts in.

    (Mr. Miller)

3. No talking in the hallway.

    (Mrs. Frazier)

4. Boys and girls, have a good day.

    (Mrs. Lucky)

5. Everybody sits at your bottom on the dot.

    (Coach Sams)

6. Clean up your table.

    (Ms. Flaky)

7. Watch if your step floor is wet.

    (The Janitor)

8. Where is your book everyone should be reading?

    (Mrs. Jason)

9. No talking until the light turns green.

    (Mr. Staff)

10. Do not forget to check in on the board.

(Mrs. Fletcher)

Tracey had a bag next to her with the prizes to pass out to the game winners. Everyone was participating. Tracey awarded the person for the correct answer after each game. Tracey has about 12 items they could choose from in the bag. She allowed them to go through the bag and pick their prizes.

The girls were enthused about correctly answering the questions and receiving a nice prize.

Mom ordered a pizza so it would be here by the time we started playing. Headache and trouble.

Someone is knocking at the door. It was the pizza man. Mom gave me the money to give the Driver. She told me to tell him no change. Tracey reached over to get the pizza from the Driver. Tracey placed the pizza in the oven until we finished playing the games.

Now it was time to play, headache and trouble. Tracey put the games on the table. The girls could choose a partner. Tracey also played with the girls to ensure enough people to play. The fun was over, and there were two winners.

Now, it was time to eat. We put up the board games. Washed up and prepared our plates.

Tracey showed everyone where the cooler was with the drinks.

Mom sat at the table with the girls. She noticed that Casey was staring at her and smiling. Mom asked her and everybody else if they were enjoying themselves. They responded yes.

Tracey's Mom did not want to get personal in asking Casey if she was OK.

That's why she asked everybody. If they were enjoying themselves. But Tracey's Mom did notice Casey was staring. Maybe Casey will share the reason when she feels more comfortable.

Everybody played the other two games on the list when they finished eating. Tracey asked everyone whether they wanted dessert.

Yes, they all replied.

Tracey asked each person what they wanted. She prepared a plate and asked them to eat it at the table.

Everyone finished eating and went into the living room to watch a movie.

Tracey asked for suggestions on what movie they wanted to see.

The girls asked Tracey if they had Netflix.

Yes, Tracey replied.

Tracey turned the Television on to Netflix and scrolled down on the screen for them to select what they wanted to look at. Several asked me to stop and press pick on a family movie.

Tracey asked if everyone agreed with the movie.

Yes, they all replied.

Everyone agreed to watch the movie together.

Mom came in with some popcorn.

I looked at everyone as they smiled when Mom walked in with the popcorn.

Thank you, the girls replied.

The movie was over. The girls cleaned the living room and went to the bedroom.

Tracey told her Mom everybody was headed to her bedroom.

"OK," Mom said.

"By the way, I have a karaoke machine. Would you like to use it?" Mom asked.

"Yes, right on time," Tracey said.

The system was in the loft with the other games. I also brought it out so the girls could play with it if they felt like it.

"I hope you all enjoy having fun with it," Mom said.

"Thanks, Mom," Tracey said.

Tracey gave her Mom a kiss and a hug.

The girls entered the bedroom with the bag of games and the Karaoke machine.

The girls wanted to play a few more games and the karaoke machine.

The girls pulled out Feeley Meeley and Mystery date game.

Tracey said these are fun games. There are no prizes.

The girls played Feeley Meeley first and Mystery Date last.

Mom came in and asked if she could play the Mystery date game. It has been some years since she played the game.

The girls allowed Mom to play first. She opened the door. Oh No, Mom opened the door, and Tracey said there was her Mystery date man, the Bum.

"That's how my luck is," Mom said.

"I'll let you girls continue playing while I do other things around the house. Have fun," Mom said.

Tracey's Mom got up and left the room.

The girls put all the board games in the bag.

Now it was time to play Karaoke.

Casey decided to be the first to use the Karaoke machine. She sang a song that sounded so good. Mom came into the room to see who was singing.

"Who is that singing?" Mom asked.

"Casey, the girls replied.

"Mom, did you hear her singing?" Tracey replied.

"Yes, I had to stop what I was doing to see who was singing that song," Mom replied.

"Yes, Casey can sing, and I heard that song before," Mom said.

Mom waited until Casey finished singing and asked her how she learned that song.

"Casey, my Mom, used to sing that song to my sister and me when we were younger," Tracey's Mom said.

"You have a beautiful voice," Mom said.

"Thank you," Casey said.

Tracey's Mom left the room and returned to what she was doing.

The girls continued to rotate the microphone and sing their hearts out.

It was getting late, so I stopped checking on the girls. I knew. Eventually, they would get sleepy. I rolled the rollaway bed close to the door and placed two sleeping bags on top of the rollaway bed just in case they wanted to sleep on the floor.

I locked the house, turned off the lights, and went to bed. About an hour I got up and checked on the girls. They all were asleep. I noticed that two girls were on the floor in sleeping bags. They did not use the roller way bed, so I moved it out.

I knew the girls would probably be sleeping late. I'm unsure if I should cook or take them out to eat breakfast at I-Hop. I will make a decision in the morning.

I got up early to check on the girls. They were still sleeping.

Around 9:00, I knocked on the door and walked into the room. The girls cleaned up and bathed to come into the kitchen for breakfast.

I cooked them a breakfast they will never forget.

I cooked grits, oatmeal, eggs, potatoes, sausage, bacon, toast, and biscuits.

They had a choice of milk, chocolate milk, or orange juice. I also made cereal available if someone did not want to eat the big breakfast. I also had some strawberries in the refrigerator for the grain cereal.

Everything was ready. The girls walked into the kitchen and said, good morning, I returned and said good morning. I asked the girls whether they slept well.

"Yes," they all replied.

"Well, girls, you can sit wherever you like. The big breakfast is on the table. Grain cereal is on the cabinet with bowls and spoons. You can serve yourself," Mom said.

Tracey asked if anyone wanted her to fix their plates.

"Yes," they replied.

Tracey went to each of her friends to ask them what they wanted for breakfast.

Tracey served her friends what they wanted for breakfast.

"Mom, do you want me to fix your plate?" Tracey asked.

"No, I already had breakfast," Mom said.

The girls finished eating, and they helped clean the kitchen.

Tracey suggested they go in the back and play basketball, hula hoop, and jump rope.

"Yes," they replied.

The girls went outside and chose what they wanted to play with. No one had to wait until someone finished playing with any of the toys. There was enough of each item to choose from.

Mom peeped out the window to check on the girls. She saw that the girls were playing pretty well with each other.

After an hour, Mom called the girls inside. She asked them to lay the toys down. She will pick them up later.

Mom said to wash up and come to the table. Mom made a picture of Lemonade and cookies.

This is right on time, Tracey said.

The time had passed by so fast. It's time to pass out the gift bags.

About 15 minutes before 12:00 p.m., Tracey went into her mom's room and got the gift bags.

The girls cleaned the kitchen and got their things together to leave. They put their bags near the front door.

Everyone was sitting in the living room, wondering where Tracey was.

Tracey returned to the living room with several gift bags in her hand.

Tracey passed out the gift bags. The girls could not wait to see what they had in their bags. They were excited to see how many items were in their gift bags for attending the slumber party.

The girls hugged Tracey for being so generous in giving them gifts, and they all had a lovely time at the slumber party.

The girls started talking about how they enjoyed themselves at the slumber party. Several of the girls mentioned how it made them feel warmed and loved.

The parents started picking up the girls. Casey was the last person to be picked up.

Tracey forgot to tell her Mom that Casey's Mom would pick her up. So she went and mentioned it to her Mom.

"Really," her Mom replied.

"Yes, her father said," Tracey said.

There was a knock at the door. Tracey answered the door. The lady said she was there to pick up Casey.

By then, Tracey's Mom had already peeped around the corner to see who was at the door. Tracey's Mom assumption was correct in thinking that Casey was her niece. Tracey's Mom played things through until a good time to let the girls know they were related.

Casey's Mom saw Tracey's Mom, and they spoke, smiled, and hugged each other.

The girls, by now, were wondering why they acted like they knew one another. Tracey thought her Mom did not hug any of the other parents. Why did she hug

Casey's Mom? Tracey was wondering what was going on. Both girls looked at one another in amazement.

Tracey's Mom said girls, we have something to tell both of you. So let's go into the living room and have a seat.

Tracey and Casey looked at each other, wondering what was going on.

The girls were thinking, are they in trouble?

We did everything right in school.

We had a lovely time at the slumber party.

Everybody got along with each other.

Tracey's and Casey's Mom asked the girls to have a seat. The girls were sitting on the opposite side of their Moms.

"Girls, this is what we want to tell both of you. Both of you are cousins ," Tracey's Mom said.

"What?" Tracey and Casey replied.

"I knew something was up. Mom, you do not just hug anybody. You acted like you knew more than you wanted to share. So I played along to see the end results, and it turned out just fine," Tracey said.

"Is this for real?" Casey asked.

"Yes, this is for real," Casey's Mom replied.

"Both of us are twins. That is why we acted the way we did. We have been out of contact for years," Tracey's Mom said.

"When Casey sang that song, I knew we were related, but I had to play things through to be sure," Tracey's Mom said.

Tracey's Mom looked at her sister and told her she was glad she was back in her life after all the years.

"Yes, I feel the same way," Casey's Mom replied.

Tracey and Casey held hands, circled, and sang Ring around the Rosie.

Casey's Mom asked the girls to sit down.

"Tracey said she was glad she had someone to play with, not just the kids at school. I had no idea I had a cousin and an auntie in the making in the same town. Wait until I get to school," Tracey said.

Yeah, I feel the same way, Casey said.

Tracey put her arms around Casey's shoulder like they had been friends for a long time.

"Casey, did you go completely through the gift bag?" Tracey's Mom asked.

"No, I figured I would pour everything out when I get home," Casey said.

"Casey, would you go get your gift bag?" Tracey's Mom asked.

"OK," Casey said.

"Here it is," Casey said.

"Look through your bag. I want to tell you something about a gift in your bag," Tracey's Mom said.

"What is this?" Casey asked.

"Open it," Tracey's Mom said.

"Mom, this is pretty," Casey said.

"Let me look at it," Casey's Mom said.

"This is Mom's locket," Casey's Mom said.

"Yes, it is. I just knew that Casey was my niece without a shadow of a doubt. I wanted to give her something she would remember: an air loom from the family. It will be left up to your Mom to ensure you take care of it," Tracey's Mom said.

"Auntie, may I give it to my Mom for safekeeping?" Casey asked.

"If you would like," Tracey's Mom said.

"Mom, I'd rather you keep this locket until I'm old enough and more responsible," Casey said.

I agree, you can wear it today, and when we get home, you can take it off. I will put it away," Casey's Mom said.

"Thank you, Auntie, for the gifts and for allowing me to attend the slumber party. We might not have met if I had not attended the slumber party," Casey said.

"I'm not so sure. I have always believed that I would see my sister again. It was a matter of time," Tracey's Mom said.

"Isn't it something how God works in mysterious ways? When you think not, he is always working in your favor," Tracey's Mom said.

EVERYBODY SAID AMEN

Printed in the United States
by Baker & Taylor Publisher Services